ALSO BY HEATHER BLANTON

Grace Be a Lady

ROMANCE IN THE ROCKIES SERIES

A Lady in Defiance

Hearts In Defiance

A Promise In Defiance

Daughter of Defiance

A Destiny in Defiance

Hope in Defiance

A Reckoning in Defiance

In Time For Christmas: A Novella

PRAISE FOR HEATHER BLANTON

"Heather Blanton infuses her stories with immense grace and dignity."

———LINDA BRODAY, *NEW YORK TIMES* BESTSELLING AUTHOR

"Heather Blanton is blessed with a natural storytelling ability, an 'old soul' wisdom, and wide expansive heart."

———MARK RICHARD, EXECUTIVE PRODUCER OF AMC'S *HELL ON WHEELS*

"Fans of Louis L'Amour and Francine Rivers will find Blanton's stories even more enthralling. With wit, a clear author's voice, and storytelling chops that rival the best—you'll have found your new favorite storyteller!"

———CARRIE FANCETT PAGELS, AWARD-WINNING AUTHOR

"Masterful at gritty fiction that points to the ultimate Creator, Heather will become one of your favorite Christian fiction authors."

———KARI TRUMBO, *USA TODAY* BESTSELLING AUTHOR

HELL-BENT ON BLESSINGS

HELL-BENT ON BLESSINGS

HEATHER BLANTON

Hell-Bent on Blessings
Paperback Edition
Copyright © 2025 (As Revised) by Heather Blanton

CKN Christian Publishing
An Imprint of Wolfpack Publishing
1707 E. Diana Street
Tampa, FL 33610

www.cknchristianpublishing.com

Paperback ISBN 979-8-89567-858-9
Ebook ISBN 979-8-89567-857-2

ACKNOWLEDGMENTS

A huge *thank you* to my editors: Vicki Prather and Lisa Coffield, and my spectacular beta readers: Becky Hrivnak, Linda Wesson, Ann Rollin, Dotty Mathison, Kaye Ferguson, Casey Heim, Jessica W, Pamela Morrisson, Cathy Egland, Rose Hale, Melissa Ahlersmeyer, Connie White, Anne Rightler, Vicki Goodwin, Liz Dent, Holly Magnuson, Janice Sisemore, Rebecca Maney, Deanna Stevens, Julia Wilson, Loraine Ertelt, Gayle Kennedy, Denise Guinn, Donita Corman, Heather Baker, Linda Brooks, Donna Walker, Jeanette shields, Jessica Woodland, Kim Buffaloe, Barb Raymond, Ruth Miller, Becky Cormier, Linda Gonzalez, Amanda Boerneke, Laura Hilton, Janice Schiefer, Britney Adams, Pam Funke, Nancy McLeroy, Jackie Ramsdell, Becky Smith, and Jennifer O'Connell!

And a huge shout-out to the awesome assistant, Becky Hrivnak! An author could not ask for a better, smarter, more dedicated support team of one. Thank you! You are such a huge blessing!

Though she be but little, she is fierce.
A Midsummer Night's Dream Act 3, Scene 2

And when she is froward, peevish, sullen, sour,
And not obedient to his honest will,
What is she but a foul, contending rebel
And graceless traitor to her loving lord?
I am ashamed that women are so simple
To offer war where they should kneel for peace,
Or seek for rule, supremacy, and sway
When they are bound to serve, love, and obey.
The Taming of the Shrew Act 5, Scene 2

— SHAKESPEARE

Love bears all things, believes all things, hopes all things, endures all things.
Love never ends.

— 1 CORINTHIANS 13:7-8 (ESV)

HELL-BENT ON BLESSINGS

CHAPTER ONE

"Momma, the sheriff's in the parlor."

Something in her thirteen-year-old daughter's voice sent a chill of foreboding up Harriet Pullen's spine, but she didn't stop her work. She slapped the whip on the ground and shook the lunge line. "Gidup, boy." The bay gelding on the other end of the rope picked up his pace to a trot and circled around her in the corral. "Good boy. Good boy." Over her shoulder to Katie, she said, "What's he want?"

"I don't know. We ran into him coming home from school and he rode on out with us. Just said he had to talk to you."

Shoot.

Harriet had much too much work to do to stop and fix another mess her worthless husband had caused. That was the only reason the sheriff ever came out here.

She sighed and slapped the whip one last time. Ricco was a good horse. Harriet was pleased with him. Willing and strong, he had heart, and he liked pleasing her. When his training was done, she would hate parting with him.

"Momma?"

Ignoring problems didn't make them go away. Harriet

lowered the whip and slowly pulled the horse around to face her, but she didn't reel him in. "You got any homework, Katie?"

"Only a little."

"All right, well..." She turned and walked the lunge line and the whip over to her daughter, who was draped over the corral fence. "Work Ricco here another fifteen minutes then put him up. Don't forget his peppermint stick. And don't get your dress dirty."

"I won't." The girl took the tools from her mother but held her gaze as their hands met. "Pa's been gone a long time, you don't think he's—"

"I'm sure he's fine." *The drunk'll probably outlive me.* "The sheriff just needs us to settle a debt for him or some such."

The girl's blue eyes cooled, and the crease in her brow said she wasn't convinced, but she nodded. "All right. And I won't forget the peppermint."

———

OUT OF HABIT, Harriet grabbed an apron off the stove's hook as she passed through the kitchen. Tying it behind her back, she marched into the parlor. Jason Meredith, Sundown's unofficial sheriff—*unofficial* because the crossroads wasn't incorporated—sat in her parlor tapping his fingertips together. A handsome man, he often wore a well-worn cowboy hat that he'd folded straight up in front, giving him an almost comic look. It sat beside him now on the settee.

Jason was certainly no man to laugh at, however. He was ridiculously tall—at least six foot six—sported a shock of hair blond as sunshine, and wielded a devastating, white, toothy smile that made most women swoon.

Harriet was immune to his soul-searching blue eyes and

strong, straight jaw, however. She was immune to men. Period. Henry had used up all her passion and kindness.

"What's he done now, Jason?" Not the politest way to start a conversation, but she was in no mood. Wrong. She was in a *foul* mood and didn't feel like dallying with niceties.

He stood slowly, much like a behemoth rising to the sky, and offered her a sad, almost embarrassed smile. "Yeah, I'm here about him."

She dropped her hands on her hips. "Do I need to bake something?" Her way of coping. It kept her from throwing things.

"Might not be a bad idea."

She stopped a worried flinch—barely—and motioned for him to follow her. "Come into the kitchen with me."

———

SHE POURED a cup of coffee and handed it to him. "Sit down. I hate looking up at you. Makes my neck hurt." He obliged, and she went to work gathering up ingredients around the kitchen for an apple pie. "Go ahead and spill it."

He glanced at the coffee. "Nah, I'd rather drink it."

She hit him with a stink eye as she plucked four eggs from a bowl on the counter and set them next to a clay crock marked *sugar*. "You know what I mean." She pulled a paring knife from the drawer, clutched another bowl to her side, this one full of apples, and joined him at the kitchen table.

He watched her hands warily as she set to peeling. "I'm not sure I want to talk to you with a knife in your hands."

Harriet didn't look up from the apple she was peeling. "Jason, I'm tired—" Unexpectedly, a lump tried to constrict her throat. She was plain worn out. Henry took her and the children two steps forward and then three back, day in and day out, and had for years. Every time they got a little ahead, he somehow managed to foul up their plans. He'd gambled away their extra cash, practically given away a good horse she'd been training, gotten arrested for drunken behavior over and over, incurring fine after fine. The last time, she'd had to bake a dozen pies for the sheriff and judge over in Whitney to cover court costs.

And this had been going on for *sixteen* years. She should be used to it by now, but she couldn't forget all the love and promise Henry had once shown. The early years of their marriage had been filled with planting dreams and watching them blossom. Then Henry had fallen into the bottle. "I'm tired of the mystery. Just tell me," she said flatly.

Jason took a sip then set the cup down. "Henry's dead."

Harriet's first thought was of the children. How would they take this? Surely they would be sad. He was their father. But he had never been a very good one, drunk more often than sober. The children were aware of the struggles the ranch endured because of his less-than-reliable behavior. So, they would be sad, yes. Devastated? She didn't think so. She certainly wasn't. She wondered what that said about the state of her conscience. Maybe she was just in shock. "How?" she heard herself ask.

"Near as anyone can tell, he drank himself to death. I guess he wandered down to the Willamette, a bottle in his hand. Just died, sitting there beside the water. But seeing as how he'd been there a while, there wasn't much to—I mean, well, identifying him took a little work. This was the clue." He pulled a gold wedding band from his breast pocket. "That is yours?"

Harriet took the ring and examined it. Engraved on the inside, it read, *To my darling Harriet. Love, Henry.* Yes, it was hers. She'd lost it a month ago but suspected all along he'd taken it to pawn.

"Are you aware he hasn't paid the mortgage in six months?"

This news hit her harder than Henry's death and froze her hands.

Oh, Henry.

She squeezed her eyes shut, despair and rising anger gripping her heart. She couldn't do *everything*. She kept up with the ranch. She raised the children. Did the shopping. Did the cooking. Balanced their ledgers. The *only* thing Henry had to do was literally pay two bills—the feedstore and bank.

Oh, Lord, please don't tell me—

She looked up and saw the sympathy in Jason's eyes. It made her feel ashamed, but not of her pragmatic thoughts. Of the man she'd married. Of her poor choice. "I counted it out every month for him. Put it in an envelope. All he had to do was walk in and hand it to the clerk."

"I guess..." He swiped a hand over his stubbly chin. "I guess he couldn't pass up the saloons. O'Dell at the bank talked to him repeatedly about it, Harriet—"

"Why didn't someone talk to me?"

"Because you're—"

"A woman?" She spat out the word, sick to death of it being equated with weakness and stupidity. "But you'll talk to me now?"

"Yes and no. I mean, you're Henry's wife, but he's legally in charge—"

She waved the knife at him. "*Was* legally in charge. You said he's dead. Before that, I hadn't seen him in almost a month. So *I'm* here to deal with things. How much does he owe the bank?"

"Well." Jason rubbed his neck and a sinking feeling lapped over Harriet like a rising tide. "It's more than the bank. He owes the feed store and a couple of merchants in town. I've been trying to put this off for you, Harriet, thinking he might come back—"

"How did you know he was gone?"

"When Henry Pullen misses more than three nights at Pauline's Parlor, everybody in this valley knows. And nobody had seen him in a month. If you'd asked, I would have looked for him."

"He came and went like he wanted. We never knew...we never knew when he was coming back." Harriet set the apple and the knife down and pressed her fingertips to her forehead, holding back a headache. "How much?"

"Unless you've got three thousand dollars, the bank is foreclosing in three days, and Bill at the feedstore is making a claim, too." He flinched a little. "And the saloon."

CHAPTER TWO

AND THE SALOON.

Three thousand dollars.

The devastating news rolled around in Harriet's head like a boulder coming down a mountain. As the rock picked up speed, so did the anger warring in her mind. Her teeth gritted and clamped together. A sneer tweaked her lips.

That man. That man. I'm going to kill him—

But he's already dead. She couldn't fathom her emotions over the news.

Jason subtly reached over and slid the knife a little further away from her. "You need to hit something, you can hit me."

The sincerity in his gaze momentarily quelled her rising fury, and, yes, the subtle sting of grief. It surprised her. Confused, floundering, she shook her head. "Do you have *any* good news for me?"

He straightened. "I think I do, actually. The bank wants the property. There's no lien on your livestock. I bet you can sell enough horses to get out from under this."

Harriet blinked. Yes, she supposed that was something.

She could sell all the horses. Give up the dream of owning a fine horse ranch and resort. To pay her worthless husband's debts. Yessirree, that was sure some good news.

On the verge of a sob, she rose and hurried to the sink, putting her back to Jason. She swallowed the lump in her throat as her eyes roamed over the great, sweeping valley that stretched out from the back door. Emerald hills and tall pines colored the view in a magical green as the Cascades rose in the distance. This was a fine place. They had built it into something. Oh, she and her young'uns still had work to do, but Whit's End Horse Farm and Ranch was establishing a respectable reputation.

"I'm sorry to deliver this kind of news on my last visit out here."

It took a moment for his statement to sink in. He'd been one of the first people Harriet had met in this valley. Always kind, seemingly interested in talking with her when they met on the street, but a perfect gentleman. She'd never felt judged by him for having married a shirker and alcoholic. Why he wasn't married was a mystery.

She turned to him. "Are you going somewhere?"

"Yes, ma'am. I'm turning in my badge and heading for Blessings."

She frowned.

"A gold town in California."

"To look for gold or sheriff?"

"Oh, I think I'm done being a sheriff for a while. Unless the Lord overrules. Otherwise, I'm going to try my hand at panning for gold."

She was remotely curious as to why he was leaving but decided not to pursue it. Gold fever had gotten hold of men from all over the country and from higher stations than sheriff. "Well, we'll miss you. You've been a good sheriff." And she would miss him.

Mouth slightly parted, he stared at her for a moment, regarding her with a serious expression. He looked as if he might say something profound but suddenly blinked it away. He rose to his feet and shrugged. "I'm sure you'll find a replacement quick. Probably won't even notice I'm gone."

She sensed that was not what he wanted to say. A little puzzled by him, she could only respond to his words at face value. "We *will* miss you. Whit and Wyatt are terribly fond of you. And I, well, I've appreciated the way you befriended the boys. They need good role models, and you have been one."

"Thanks. They're good boys. They'll be all right." Jason raised a hand to his hip and licked his lips. "You know, I hear there's plenty of jobs in those boomtowns. I bet you could make a good living down there in Blessings."

Her brow arched. "Washing tattered long johns? Serving slop to drunk miners?" How could he even sugge—?

"Just an idea. If you get, you know, sideways of the bank or something."

"Sounds like I already am." He flinched, and she let out a long, slow breath. He didn't deserve this slicing tongue of hers. "I'm sorry, Jason. I just hope I don't get that desperate. Good luck to you in California."

He took her hand and looked deeply into her eyes, surprising her with his intensity. Again, she had the sense he wanted to say more than what came out of his mouth. "May God bless and keep you, Harriet. I'll miss you, too."

With that, he slipped back through the parlor, snatched his hat up off the settee, and strode from the house, long legs carrying him out in three steps. The slam of the screen door announced his final exit. She closed her hand, the one he'd held, marveling over the warmth she still felt.

———

FROM THE BACKYARD, Harriet heard her two teenage sons fussing about chores and took a deep breath. What was she going to do? She loved this ranch. It kept her sane. Her eyes roamed over the kitchen, the knick-knack shelf, the pie ingredients on the counter. She would bake and think…then maybe go for a ride and think some more.

"You are so lazy." Whit's aggravated voice floated through the screen door behind her.

She picked up the knife and the bowl of apples and slogged outside to the back porch. "You two quit your fussing and get your chores done."

The boys looked up from the sack of feed they were wrestling up into the back of the feed wagon. "He's not carrying his weight, Ma." Whit, her seventeen-year-old, fumed and punched his brother on the shoulder. "He's letting me do all the work." Tall, good-looking, and lean as a bean pole, he swept dusty-blond hair out of his eyes and glared at his little brother. "Carry your weight."

His boyish looks hinted at the handsome man waiting in the wings and Harriet smiled a little sadly. Wyatt, only fourteen, was the opposite of Whit in every way possible. Shorter, built like a bull moose, with bear paws for hands, he was as peaceful as an old hound dog. Nothing riled Wyatt. Nothing built up steam in him—except his older brother.

He slammed down his end of the feed on the tailgate of the wagon and glared right back at Whit. "I *was* carrying my weight."

"Sure felt like I was doing all the work—"

"Boys, enough," Harriet interrupted firmly. "Go feed the cows then come back and put Ricco up for Katie." Her daughter was still out in the corral lunging the horse. His empty back, however, called to Harriet like a siren's song. "On second thought, I'm gonna take him for a ride. I'll make the pie when I get back."

She had some thinking to do, and she was never clearer than when she was in the saddle. Loping across the green hills of her ranch, she could figure out her next steps.

CHAPTER THREE

"I've got two days, Beth. Two days to make some decisions." Harriet couldn't drink the coffee. She slid the cup away and stared up at a shelf in her sister's kitchen—a ledge lined with dainty blue and white china. "The bank gave me a flat-out no. No extra time. No extension on the loan. Henry used up all their good graces. I swear, if he wasn't dead I'd kill him. I don't have the money to pay off these debts. We're going to lose everything."

Beth sat down opposite her, violet eyes shimmering with tears. "I'm so sorry you're going through this, Harriet. I'll do anything I can to help you."

She knew Beth meant it. Harriet had always been able to rely on her older sister. She took a deep breath, willing to share the glimmer of an idea. "You know, Jason left for a boomtown called Blessings. He's going to pan for gold. He told me there's plenty of work down there."

"I've heard that, too. Those towns need women—*decent* women—to cook and sew and clean. And they pay top dollar. Eliza Morton went out to Eureka, I think it was. She made enough money to open a boarding house there."

"Really?" That was intriguing.

"Are you thinking about leaving Oregon for California?" The shake in Beth's tone betrayed concern.

"Mmm...well..." Harriet hemmed and hawed, bobbing her head from left to right. "Maybe. At least, I wanted to toss out an idea."

Beth flicked a long, dark braid over her shoulder and laced her fingers together. Down to business. "All right."

"I have to let the bank have the ranch. I don't have any choice. I can sell Ricco and pay off the account at the feed store and a few other smaller accounts. I've decided I'm not going to pay the saloon."

"I don't blame you there. They knew Henry's reputation. But without the ranch, what are you going to do? Where are you going to live?"

"Beth, I can keep two things out of this mess." She leaned forward and took her sister's hand. "My children and my horses. But I can't keep them with me. At least not if I go to California. I'd need to leave them with you for a little while."

"Of course, but what are you thinking about doing?"

"When I was at the feed store, I read the notice board. There really *are* a lot of jobs in the mining towns."

Beth sagged a little. "Hard work. But plenty of men. You'll be married in a year."

Harriet pursed her lips and pulled away. She swore she could feel her heart turn to lead. "Oh, no, I won't. I've had enough of men. They're not worth the burden...or the heartache."

Her mind ticked off all the times Henry had fallen asleep at the dinner table or wasn't sober enough to settle simple disputes between the boys. Or didn't have the concentration or gumption to finish even small projects around the ranch. If it hadn't been for the boys helping, the place would have fallen into complete disrepair. But when they were old enough to hold a hammer, Harriet had put them to work saving her dream.

And she'd lost it anyway.

A ferocious resolve rose up in her. "I'm done, Beth. From now on, I'll make it on my own. I'll never rely on a man again...not for anything."

Her sister's brow pinched with, Harriet knew, a little sadness. "Why don't we just take this one day at a time? So you're going to go get a job?"

"Yes, I think so. I hope it won't be for long. Whit and Wyatt can take care of the horses while I'm gone. I'll save as much money as I can, as fast as I can. Then send for them. Katie may stay with you longer, Beth. When I'm convinced the town is decent and safe, or I move to one that is. Eventually, I'll send for the horses and we'll start over."

From a plug of dirt, if I have to, but I will start over and get my dream and my children back.

"But what town? Where are you going? I think you should follow Jason."

"Follow Jason? Well, I..."

"Why not? Any gold rush town could be dangerous. Rowdy. Lawless. You should know a man there, especially one who used to wear a badge."

"I don't know..." Harriet squirmed at the idea. "I wouldn't want him to think I followed him—"

"Who cares what he thinks? It would be better for you to know someone in a strange, new town. You can't argue with that."

"No, I suppose it's not an awful idea. Blessings, huh?"

CHAPTER FOUR

HARRIET HAD NEVER DEALT WITH HEARTACHE BY SLATHERING IT in anger, at least not before Henry had become such a disappointment. He had taught her the trick. She finished braiding her long blonde locks then took a deep breath and a good long look at herself in the mirror. Her green eyes glittered with too much determination, she held her chin too high, her lips pursed too tightly. Good grief, she looked—no, *radiated*— she *radiated* anger. This was no way to say goodbye to her children.

Harriet flung her braid behind her and rolled her shoulders, trying to erase the tension.

This is NOT goodbye, Harriet. You'll see Whit, Wyatt, and Katie soon. Her face hardened again. *In fact, the harder you work, the faster you'll see them.*

Oh, and she would. She would work like Lucifer himself was breathing down her neck. She would see her children sooner rather than later, and nothing was going to get in her way. Blessings had better open up and spill every opportunity it cradled right into her lap if the town knew what was good for it.

Once more, she tried to lighten her countenance by pasting on a strained smile, then marched out to tell her children goodbye. All three of them waited for her beside the wagon. Beth sat in the driver's seat, clenching the reins in her hands. The sight of her family—their downcast expressions and shining eyes—squeezed Harriet's heart and her knees almost buckled. This was Henry's doing. Lord, how she could throttle that man if he were standing here.

She forced the ugly thought away and swallowed the knot in her throat. "No hangdog faces now." Approaching them, she touched their noses in turn and sighed. "This isn't goodbye, just so long. For a spell. I'll get us squared away. Then, Whit, you and Wyatt will join me. Katie, I—" Tears spilled down her daughter's cheeks and Harriet clenched her jaws together, battling for control of her face and her emotions. "Katie, now—" No, it was no good. Harriet's voice broke and she pulled her daughter into a tight embrace. Whit and Wyatt wrapped their arms around them and the tears ran freely.

Harriet shook her head and hugged her children. The embraces were breath-stealing, desperately tight. It would take everything in her to leave now. But she had to. So that this very situation didn't repeat itself. She would never, ever let a man hold the power of the purse strings over her again. Harriet's home, her children, and her livelihood would be in her own hands going forward.

"Harriet, are you sure...?" Beth whispered from her seat above them. "You know you're welcome to stay here."

For a moment, her children's tears and unsure expressions could have swayed her. But Harriet would die on this tiny farm, living off her sister's charity. And besides, Beth hated horses. Was terrified of them ever since she'd been thrown as a child.

No, a little pain now would bring them greater joy and stability in the future—if Harriet could make this dream come true. She only knew she would dig her heels in and try with all her might.

Feeling as if she were ripping out her own heart, she stepped back, unwillingly letting the arms of her children fall away. She stared into their misery-laden faces. "If there was another way that would bring us a good life, get our independence back, start the ranch over, I would do it. You know that." They didn't respond. "Right?" She *needed* their approval. Slowly, they nodded. She looked up at Whit. Seemed he'd sprung up overnight and now the boy towered over her. "I bet I'll surprise you how soon I can send for you." She scanned Wyatt's and Katie's tear-streaked faces. "All three of you."

Whit laid his hand on her shoulder. "Do what you have to do, Ma. We'll be all right. I'll take care of Wyatt and Katie and we'll help out around here. Don't worry so much about us."

She closed her eyes to absorb his calm determination. He was trying to make this easier for her. And she loved him for his courage. "You know the horses make Aunt Beth nervous. Work with them every day."

"I will. I'll work with them so much, they'll have the manners of English lords when you see 'em next."

She thrust her hand out and the two grabbed each other's wrists like Indians. "I'll hold you to that."

———

AFTER AN ALMOST PLEASANT voyage to San Francisco, Harriet's travel turned miserable. The stage, stuffed with miners and men in fine suits—gamblers, Harriet supposed—slogged through torrential rain and mud six inches deep for two days. She wondered if the deluge would ever quit. It had rained so hard at one point, rivulets of water wound their way through the roof of the stage and dripped onto her shoulder. She'd changed seats, stepping over backpacks loaded with tin pans and picks. Watched intently by the male passengers, she squeezed in between the wall and a young man who had thus far slept most of the trip, his head lolling with the sway of the stage.

Wishing she could find such peace, Harriet peeled the canvas curtain back and looked out at the gray rain and deep green evergreens passing by. A damp cold sank into her bones.

"Blessings, three miles," the driver called, his voice muffled by the soggy atmosphere.

Her heart suddenly pounded in her chest. Had she made a mistake? Should she have stayed in the Willamette Valley? But she could make twice the money here cooking and cleaning as opposed to wages for the same drudgery back home. This had to be a wise move. But what if she couldn't find a job? Oh, that was ludicrous. Of course, she'd find a job—

Stop it, Harriet! Square your shoulders, raise your chin, and go do what you have to do to get your children and your life back.

CHAPTER FIVE

WHEN THE STAGECOACH PULLED INTO BLESSINGS, HARRIET AND the other passengers disembarked into a steady, depressing drizzle. Men, horses, mules, and wagons surged about them in the boomtown. Dingy tents swayed in the breeze, water poured off the roofs of a few newer clapboard buildings. The street was a quagmire of mud and the wagons rolling by made deep, sucking sounds in it.

"Not much of a town, is it," the young man mumbled from beside her, flapping water off his lapels. A pointless move, she thought, as water cascaded down the back of his hat.

The saloon, the closest building, had a porch but no roof. Harriet lifted her skirt, resigned to the drowning, and headed for it. "Perhaps it will get better." She hurried to the landing, happy at least to be out of the mud, and turned to the driver, who was atop the stage, tugging at the stack of luggage. "Driver, can you tell me where the hotel is?"

"Yes, ma'am, about two hours back, in Culloma." He tossed her bag at her. She had to sidestep to avoid being hit by it and it thunked in the mud. "Sorry, ma'am."

She picked it up quickly. *Two hours?* This information did not sit well with Harriet. "Well, where do visitors stay?"

Seemingly oblivious to the weather, the man paused and scratched his head. "Well, ma'am, I reckon most of 'em stake a claim and pitch a tent."

Disheartened, Harriet took a halting step backward. She had seven dollars to her name. She didn't know anyone in town—well, there was Jason, but she had no idea how to find him. And there was no hotel.

Through the rain, she saw a tent across the road. A makeshift mercantile or trading post of sorts, she guessed, by the plethora of items sitting out front getting wet. Shovels, picks, hammers, lanterns, and other items decorated the front entrance.

The inside of the tent would be dry, and it was better than the saloon. She blinked water out of her eyes. If she could get dry, she could think more clearly. She realized then the young man from the stage was making a beeline through the mud to the tent. Whether it looked like she was following him or not didn't matter a whit to Harriet. She wanted to be dry. Hiking her skirt up, she charged for the little mercantile, the amber glow from the interior calling to her.

"Just up and quit, the ol' crotchety fart."

Harriet burst into the tent and two men, talking over a barrel, stopped their conversation abruptly and surveyed her no doubt bedraggled appearance. She gulped. "I'm sorry. I didn't mean to interrupt." The tent was small, the quarters close. The young man from the stagecoach stood toward the back, his bag at his feet, peeling off his hat and coat, paying her no mind.

"No worries," a tall, thin man said with a heavy Australian accent. He pointed at the man on the other side of the barrel. "Dundee here was just complaining about his cook up and quittin'. Twenty cold, wet, hungry carpenters ain't going to have a meal waiting when they come in from building the wharf."

Dundee turned to face her, a corncob pipe hanging from the corner of his mouth. Wearing a pair of gold spectacles, he was a short, bookish-looking man, but thick as a Carolina oak and topped with thick, gray hair. Scowling, his dark eyes gave Harriet a mildly interested perusal. "Willoughby here misspeaks." He motioned toward the first man. "The bloke didn't *quit*." An Australian accent painted his every syllable as well. "He's lying in the bushes somewhere, drunk as a skunk. And he's also about as employed as a skunk." He regarded Harriet with a sudden intensity. "You lookin' for work?"

Her mouth fell open. Could it be this easy? "Desperately."

The pipe slipped from Dundee's mouth, but he scrambled and caught it before it hit the ground. "Truly? Do you cook?" He sounded flabbergasted at his luck, but then his hand sliced the air with the pipe. "Mind you, I ain't askin' if you cook *well*. Just can you cook?"

"I cook well. I bake even better."

Both men's eyes bugged, then Dundee shoved the pipe back into his mouth and lifted his chin. "Three dollars a week?"

"Five and you'll have a fine, *reliable* cook."

Dundee didn't hesitate. He shoved out his hand. "I'm Michael James Dundee, entrepreneur. Everyone calls me Dundee. This week, I'm in construction. Got me a crew building a wharf on Prospect Creek. My businesses may vary, sometimes day to day, but I always need a cook. Three squares a day, seven days a week."

Harriet would have preferred six days but wouldn't push her luck. The man had given her five dollars a week. She would get more…later. And she would cook extra on Saturdays to make the work light on Sundays. All in all, this might be a fine arrangement. She shook Dundee's hand and nodded. "Agreed."

———

MICHAEL JAMES DUNDEE hailed from Brisbane and explained to Harriet, as they hurried through the mud and rain, that he'd come to California to make his fortune. "But not in gold," he explained, bustling toward a group of tents. "In what these tinhorn forty-niners need to *get* their gold."

"Speaking of needs, Dundee." Harriet hustled to keep up with the little man's quick stride. "I need a place to stay. Do you know of—"

"There's a tent right behind the kitchen. It's yours. I'll toss out the worthless lickspittle's belongings, and you can move right in."

Things were moving along at a breakneck pace but, considering the hopelessness that had been dogging her heels only a few minutes ago, Harriet was encouraged. She had employment and a place to stay. Her spirits lifted considerably with the sense of security.

And then she saw the kitchen...

Dundee's use of the word bordered on an obscene lie. This *kitchen* consisted of a tarp pulled across some logs that, because of hanging hams and heavy sides of bacon, drooped so low she and her new employer literally had to bend over to enter, and there was not enough room to stand upright once inside. Adding to the misery, the previous chef had left the dirt floor littered with food scraps and two long plank tables buried under a mountain of dirty plates.

Air, and perhaps all her hope, whooshed out of Harriet as if she'd been punched in the stomach.

Dundee cleared his throat and shrugged. "It ain't much, but there's the stove"—he pointed quickly around them—

"pantry is under that counter, fresh water in the barrel. Have supper ready at six." Before Harriet could say anything, he ducked back out into the rain, yelling over his shoulder, "I'll have Magruder's things cleaned out shortly. His tent's right there." A jerk of his thumb and he was gone.

Bowed by the swaybacked tent, Harriet shuffled over to the stove and touched it. Ice cold.

Rivulets of water spiraled down her hair, dripped on her back, dribbled inside her shirtwaist. A chill hit her as she surveyed the filthy floor, alive with pleasantly stuffed roaches. Her gaze drifted to the table, blue tin plates stacked helter-skelter, most still covered in food and sporting their own tribes of insects.

Suddenly, with brutal surprise, a sob escaped, nearly driving her to her knees. She stumbled to a box and collapsed. The question *what have I done, what have I done* kept echoing through her mind. Oh, how she missed her children. Her ranch. Her horses. Her...simple life.

*Oh, God...*she hid her face in her hands and wept, overcome with fear and doubt. *I'm so afraid.*

You have a job and a place to sleep.

Harriet sat up and looked around the tent. A voice. She had clearly heard a voice. However, aside from the gentle pulse of the rain and the traffic from Blessings' Main Street several hundred yards away, she was alone.

She replayed the voice. A man's voice, gentle and calming, but it hadn't been accusatory or angry.

Stress, she told herself. *I'm overwrought with everything. That's all.* The explanation didn't ring true. Harriet hadn't prayed in years. Hadn't really prayed a little while ago when she'd gotten off the stage, but something in her had cried out to God. She couldn't deny that. And when the job had fallen into her lap, she'd...felt something. Like a calm assurance that she wasn't alone.

Had He heard a half-formed prayer? Had He heeded a desperate heart?

Harriet once again surveyed this mess that masqueraded as a kitchen. Yes, it was awful. But she was dry. She could start a fire and get warm. She could use the ashes from the fireplace to scrub the dishes. Then she would cook and make more money in a day than she could make in a week back home. And she would be thankful, no matter the conditions.

Yes, Lord, I am trying.

Wiping away her tears, Harriet rose and rolled up her sleeves. Her heart nearly leaped out of her chest when she realized Jason Meredith was standing outside in the rain watching her, an expression of compassion and pity creasing his brow.

She flushed with humiliation and clenched her jaws. "What are you doing here?" she snapped.

He joined her in the tent and removed his hat but couldn't straighten up. Much taller than she, the low roof had him nearly doubled over. "I, uh, heard from Roderick Parker you were coming to Blessings." He frowned at the tarp forcing him to hunch his shoulders as the water cascaded off his leather duster. "And I heard today that Magruder had walked out on Dundee. I thought I might see if he was of a mind to hold the job for you. And here you are. Did he hire you?" He twirled his waterlogged cowboy hat in his hands, waiting for an answer.

Harriet sagged, relaxing her shoulders. Again, Jason had done nothing to deserve this ire, other than be born a man. "I'm sorry. There's no call for my rudeness...I'm just...done-in, Jason, to be honest." The confession surprised her, but it was the truth. Her supply of hope was at a dangerous low despite the way the Lord seemed to be involved. "Maybe things will be better now. Yes, he hired me. I have a job making five dollars a week. That's a step in the right direction."

"It is. Anything I can do to help? You need anything?"

From a man? She wanted to spit. "No. I'm fine now. Squared away. You needn't worry about me." Or stop by again. His presence taxed her somehow. Made her feel weepy again, and vulnerable. She wished he'd leave so she could withdraw into herself and get to the work at hand.

He grunted softly and dropped his hat back in place. Though he looked uncertain for a moment, he flashed her that sugary, sideways grin. "All right, I'm sure you'll be fine. But if you need anything…"

"Thank you."

She left it at that and he seemed to sense the dismissal. With an awkward nod, he slipped back out into the rain.

CHAPTER SIX

Jason didn't know what he'd been expecting from her, but when Harriet's jade eyes had fallen on him, he thought he'd seen a little relief at meeting an old friend. *And then she saw that worthless, no-good husband of hers.*

He shrugged his shoulders to shake off the water from his duster but realized the futility of the action. As he strode along the pine-needle carpet toward his claim down on the creek, he wondered if she'd ever let go of the hurt.

Ma hadn't. Marrying the wrong man had done her in too, and hardened her, like a brick baked in the sun. That was happening to Harriet and he hated it. Somehow, he had to make her believe all men were not Henry Pullen.

He supposed the only option was patience. After all, he'd left for Blessings in an attempt to distance himself from her. Clear his head. The discovery of Henry's death had nearly talked him into staying. But, no, he'd prayed about moving on and felt led to be here. And now here *she* was.

"That's no coincidence, Lord," he whispered as the rain finally sputtered to a stop. "Maybe she followed me, and she just doesn't know it yet." He smiled wryly. That would be just like a woman. Just like Harriet. She didn't exactly ease into situations that weren't her idea. "Grant me patience, Lord, grant me patience."

"Jason," a voice hailed him and he turned to the left, where the trail broke off and headed for Main Street.

He saw a long, lanky figure hurrying toward him. Gangly arms and legs moved with surprising fluidity, like a bug. Only one man in Blessings resembled a praying mantis. Archie Reives. Calling himself an entrepreneur, he was currently running a small shipping operation on the river.

Jason lifted a hand. "Reives."

"Jason, buddy." Reives hurried up to him and unfolded a long arm, grabbing Jason's shoulder. "Glad I caught you. We're having a little shindig on the boat this evening. Thought you might like to come...as my special guest."

Jason knew full well Reives's idea of a shindig was a cash bar on the water. He wanted someone on the boat capable of controlling rowdy drunks. Well, Jason wasn't in law enforcement anymore. He had a nice little claim down by the water that was giving up its wealth little by little. Nothing grand, but he was going to leave Blessings with a fine stash. Maybe several thousand dollars. He kept this information, however, close to the vest.

"No thanks, Reives. 'Preciate the offer, though."

Reives was not a man to beg. A bony jaw that tightened a little and bland, hazel eyes that narrowed some were the only signs he disapproved of Jason's answer. "Maybe next time, then. You change your mind, your first drink is on me." He started to walk away but stopped abruptly. "You know, I'm planning on being a big man in Blessings." He hooked his thumbs into his belt loop and rocked on his heels. "It wouldn't hurt you to get on my good side."

Jason had heard veiled threats like this plenty of times back in Washington and Oregon. Little men who thought they were big men, overestimating their girth. He shrugged, not intimidated. "I'll keep that in mind."

Of course, even a little rattlesnake could kill you.

———

ONCE THE FIRE had caught and the stove in the center of the tent had started emitting some heat, Harriet's spirits rose again. By four-thirty, she had a clean kitchen, apple pies cooling and more in the oven, and a huge pot of stew simmering on top. She set a stack of tin bowls at the end of the plank tables, placed two coffee cans full of silverware beside them, and stepped over to stir the stew.

"Mrs. Pullen, you've worked wonders."

She spun, spoon in hand, at the astonishment in Dundee's voice. "Yes, I'd say getting this kitchen functioning again was nigh unto a miracle." She scowled at him. "It took an act of God to run out the roaches."

"Ah, well." He shrugged, looking a little embarrassed. "No worries. He's in the business of starting and stopping plagues, eh?"

Harriet lifted an eyebrow, not amused by the flippant comment. Cleaning this mess had nearly killed her. The roaches had made her skin crawl as she chased them, stomped them, and flicked them off the plates into the stove. A shiver shot down her spine. She hated roaches. "And I'm in the business of cooking and running a clean kitchen. Your men will have a fine meal, but I'll expect them to wash in that barrel over there before they sit down."

Dundee eyed the container skeptically then nodded. "Fine. I'll make sure they know. They should all be here any minute."

And in minutes, Harriet found herself flooded with an army of hungry men. They squeezed into the plank tables, jabbering excitedly and eyeing her with clear expectations.

"Bet you'll put Magruder to shame," one man called.

"If she doesn't," another said, "who cares. She's nicer to look at."

A rumble of laughter circled the tables as Harriet served stew to the waiting men. A fellow with white-blond hair held up his bowl and smiled tenderly. "Dundee says you're a widow. Is that true?"

Harriet was surprised by the question and her scoop paused. "Yes, I am, but how did he know that?"

"Ain't you friends with Jason Meredith? He told Dundee a little about you."

She dumped the spoon. "Oh, I see."

Harriet couldn't serve the food fast enough. It seemed as soon as she passed around one entrée, bowls were rising in the air for seconds. Turned out, though, the showstopper was her apple pie.

"Holy cow," one of the carpenters whispered after taking a bite. "That's better than my beloved mother's."

When the last piece slid onto a plate, a miner at the head of the other table held up a gold nugget. "Mrs. Pullen, I will give you a gold nugget worth fifty dollars if you'll bake me a pie just like this one."

Harriet blinked and had the urge to clean her ear. She couldn't have heard him right. Yet, the man held the gold, waiting. Momentarily, she gave the man a warm grin and reached for the nugget.

———

ABSENTLY CLEARING A TABLE, Harriet was making plans for pies and meals when Dundee approached her, trailed by two men. Building a stack of dishes on her arm, she straightened— as much as the tent allowed—and placed the stack of dirty plates back on the table. "Dundee."

"Mrs. Pullen, I heard dinner was a rousing success. I came for leftovers, but the way the men were raving, I suspect there are none."

"I hardly have to wash the dishes. Your boys nearly *licked* them clean."

He chuckled. "I think I've hired a fine cook. Thank you. And these boys"—he motioned over his stooped shoulders—"are going to fix this ramshackle tent so you can stand up straight in here and cook proper-like."

"Well, *that* would be nice." Harriet rubbed her aching back. "And I'm looking forward to seeing my new home soon." She had yet to look in the tent where she would be staying, but it didn't matter. Short bed bugs or more roaches, she was sleeping anywhere…even on her feet if necessary.

"We moved Magruder's belongings over to the trading post. Tent's all ready for ya. Well, there's no blankets or anything of the sort, but you can use this—" Dundee reached into his breast pocket and pulled out a five-dollar bill. "This is for you. A week's pay in advance. Buy some essentials from the mercantile."

"Oh, my." Harriet took the money, surprised by the man's generosity. "You didn't have to—"

"And you are happy with the five dollars a week?"

"Dundee!"

Harriet jumped at the gravelly voice bellowing from the falling darkness outside.

Dundee grimaced and wiped a hand over his face. "Guess the dingle found his belongings."

A middle-aged man, about as tall as he was wide and dressed in slovenly, wrinkled clothes, charged into the tent. "Whatta you mean throwing my bag on the porch at the trading post?"

"You left me with a crew to feed and you were nowhere in sight, you drunken wombat. You're fired!"

"Fired?" The man's brows dove and he snatched at the bill in Harriet's hand. On her guard, she was faster and clutched the bill to her bosom.

"That's my pay," the sot bellowed.

"You dink," Dundee stepped between them and shoved the man back. "I'll have your guts in a frying pan, you try anyth—"

Magruder tossed a punch at Dundee and sent him flying back against the stove.

"Stop this," Harriet screamed, ready to kill someone if this fight messed up her kitchen.

Before Dundee could recover, Jason appeared from nowhere, charging into the tent like an angry bull. He nailed Magruder with a vicious right hook, sending the former cook stumbling back, arms pinwheeling crazily. He crashed into the plank table, sending the dirty bowls clattering to the ground in a cacophony of metal. The two men who had accompanied Dundee stepped forward, coming alongside Jason.

Magruder righted himself as much as possible under the low roof and glared at Jason but didn't ignore the odds. He spat at Dundee's feet. "You owe me, Dundee. You owe me."

Rubbing his jaw, Dundee glared at the cook. "Mate, you're a buffoon and a drunken one at that. I don't owe you a dime. Get out of my kitchen."

Ready to enforce the eviction, Jason and the other two men inched forward, fists raised. Magruder spat again and stormed out of the tent.

Harriet let out a breath she hadn't even known she'd been holding. "I think you may still be in law enforcement, Jason."

A wry smile tipped his lips. "Looks more like personal security to me."

Harriet couldn't help herself. She smiled back. The man had ended what could have been an ugly affair resulting in her being back to seven dollars instead of the twelve. She scanned the men before her. "I was holding back one apple pie, gentlemen. Would you like to share it?"

The nods and smiles almost made Harriet forget about Magruder stomping down the trail. He glanced back, and their eyes met. Fear wriggled in her stomach. On second thought, maybe he would have done something worse than take her money.

Yes, having a friend like Jason in Blessings probably wasn't a bad thing at all.

CHAPTER SEVEN

HARRIET'S PIES QUICKLY BECAME THE TALK OF BLESSINGS. MEN approached her before the wharf crew swarmed the tables to bribe food from her. Rather than dismiss the requests, she told them to come back later. If it was all right with Dundee, she'd make extra and sell them a meal or a pie.

Initially, Dundee said no, but a few days later he wandered into the kitchen tent, hands behind his back, a thoughtful expression on his face. Rolling out dough for turnovers, Harriet greeted him but kept working. "Good morning, Dundee."

"Good morning, Mrs. Pullen." He wandered aimlessly around the kitchen for a moment, picking up knives, examining tin plates.

"Something on your mind, Dundee?"

"Meals." He laid down a fork and turned to her. "Men all over Blessings are commenting on your food, Mrs. Pullen. They want to buy meals from us. How would you feel about running an extra shift?"

An extra shift? Her back ached at the thought, but...more

money meant she would see her children that much faster. "Just one. With a raise."

————

HARRIET COOKED LIKE A WOMAN POSSESSED. Dundee indeed added one dinner shift, available after his crew ate. Only able to feed another twenty or so men, she turned away at least that many every day. Any more and she was going to demand a waitress and a larger pantry. But pies—those she could sell hot, cold, or in between. And she took orders, at least a dozen every day.

Along with the pies, the faces of the men in Blessings blurred in front of her as she kneaded, fried, flipped, seared, and served. Beards and plaid shirts and throaty laughter melted into one nondescript forty-niner or river wharf carpenter.

No. Not true. One unique face showed up every night, and he was always early, to be sure to get a seat. Jason Meredith didn't miss a meal.

He leaned out of the way so Harriet could drop mashed potatoes onto his plate. "Evening, Jason."

"Evening, Harriet. What's on the menu tonight?"

"Mashed potatoes and elk steaks." While she served the potatoes, the trays stacked with the steaks circulated around the tables. "Not my favorite, but we had a hunter trade them for some pies."

"Half the town is trying to eat here just for those pies."

"And what about you? What are you here for?"

She had meant it innocently enough, but the question seemed to trip him up. His blue eyes widened and a grin alternated with a shocked *o* on his mouth.

Harriet laughed at his awkwardness. "Steaks or pies?"

"What?"

"Are you here for the steaks or pies?"

"Um..." He shook his head and let the grin win. "The pies. I'm definitely here for the pies."

"All right. Blueberry tonight."

―――――

ONE THING inherent in this new profession of Harriet's was the availability of gossip. As she moved among the men, she heard everything from who had struck it rich, to what new businesses had come into town, to who wanted to run for mayor if Blessings ever got that organized.

Tonight, as she poured coffee for Jason, the man next to him said the most intriguing thing of all. "A shipping company. Yes, sir." He stabbed his shepherd's pie as if it had offended him. "That's what Blessing needs now. There's plenty of folks here now who need stuff."

"I don't see any horses," Jason said, sounding half-interested. He nodded a thanks at Harriet for the coffee and added, "Nothing around here but skinny nags. Mules and horses are the first thing you need for freighting. Good, strong ones, well-trained. I used to drive a wagon. A poorly trained horse will toss you over a mountainside faster than a peeved grizzly."

But Harriet didn't really hear any of that. She was stuck on *good, strong ones, well-trained.*

Like her horses back on Beth's farm.

―――――

LATER THAT NIGHT, the tables cleared and six pies baking in the oven, Harriet sat down in her tent and dumped a box out on her bed. Bills and coins spilled across her wool blanket.

She split the profit on the pies with Dundee, but she also

had her wages—now *seven* dollars a week. A quick count showed she had made nearly one hundred dollars in three weeks. She needed at least twice that, but she was closer—

"Harriet?"

Jason? Puzzled by his unexpected visit, she raked the money into the box. "Yes, come in." She finished tidying up the money and rose to meet him. "It's late, what are you doing here?"

He snatched off that ridiculously folded hat. "The whole town smells like apple and cherry pies, so I knew you were still up baking."

"Yes." She shrugged. "Twenty pies ordered for tomorrow."

"Yeah, I need to get in on that." His gaze drifted to the box in her hand. "You got enough yet, to bring the boys and Katie to Blessings?"

"A few dollars more to go and I'll get the boys first. I want to be more established before I bring a young lady into a boomtown. To that end, I was thinking about something..."

"The shipping company?"

"How did you know?"

"Umm, there's a look you get when you're planning on throwing something...or you're planning."

"They're the same?"

"Yeah." He tapped a spot between her eyes. "You get a funny little *v* right there." His touch made her suddenly aware of him. How tall and handsome and strong. He cleared his throat and moved back an inch. "I couldn't recall anything that had made you mad, so I figured it was the comment on the freighting and the horses that had you planning."

"So you think it's a bad idea?"

"Opening a shipping company? No, I think it's a great idea. I think the bad idea is doing it on your own."

Harriet sucked in a breath, a coal of anger glowing to life. "Who do you think you—"

"Calm down." Jason patted the air. "And don't reach for anything to throw. Opening a business is a lot of work, especially one you don't know anything about. But you know horses. I know freighting."

Harriet shifted her weight to one foot and tilted her chin to show her disapproval. "I don't need your help. If I want to open a freight business, I will. I can drive a wagon, and I can handle my horses."

"You don't know anything about harnesses for long-distance hauling, the right wagons to use for different terrain, or how to pair horses up for speed and power. You need to ride the trails before you take your wagons over them so you don't get stuck somewhere or, worse, wear out your horses."

That got her attention. She'd never want to foolishly risk her stock.

Jason tapped his chest with the hat. "I'm proposing a business deal."

"What kind of business deal?"

"I want to be your partner."

"No." The refusal had leaped out of her mouth before she'd actually thought about it. Still… "No. I don't want a partner."

"Why?"

She didn't want the complication, the entanglement. She didn't want a *man* around. But mostly, she just didn't want a partner *because* she didn't need any help. And that struck her as something Katie would say while stomping her foot.

"You should be smart about this, Harriet. Don't let your pride get in your way."

She chewed on the idea for a moment. Jason had made some good points. "If"—she jabbed her index finger heavenward—"*if* I were interested, what were you thinking?"

CHAPTER EIGHT

HARRIET HELD THE TENT FLAP AND LISTENED TO JASON whistling a jaunty tune as he slipped away into the night. *Well, he's certainly happy about the arrangement.*

They'd agreed on a sixty-forty split, after his initial investment was paid back. Jason would purchase two new wagons, the harnesses, and rent a barn to function as the headquarters. He would also dispatch a reliable man to fetch the boys and her horses and bring them up via ship. The mere thought of the future reunion moved her to tears.

Things had moved much faster than she'd dared hope. She wanted to throw open her arms and spin around like a child. Instead, choking with gratitude, she looked up at the glittering night sky. "Thank You," she whispered. "Thank You."

———

"YOU CAN'T BRING the boys and Katie up here if you don't have a real place to live, Harriet."

Hands over her eyes, Jason had carefully guided her for several minutes without a clue as to where they were going.

Until just then. "What do you mean, Jason? The tent is fine. I've got money saved. I'll be able to afford a cabin soon now."

"Sooner."

"What?" She stumbled on the uneven ground, but somehow, he kept her upright.

"Easy does it. Just a few more steps." He stopped, pulling her to a halt. The strong scent of fresh pine tickled her nose and she liked it. "Ta-da," he whispered in her ear, his warm breath on her skin actually giving her goose bumps, then he pulled his hands away. "Your new home."

A one-room cabin with a porch greeted her. A new structure, it still held the gleam and smell of fresh-cut lumber. The home had glass in the windows, a river rock fireplace on the side, and a large, flat stone in front of the porch for a step.

"I don't understand, Jason. Is this mine?"

"You're renting it. I made a deal with Atherton Winslet for it. I told him you still hadn't found a place you could afford. We negotiated the rent down to something palatable."

Harriet clutched her hands over her heart. A home. A wood floor beneath her feet. She didn't care what it cost. She didn't care if she had to bake two hundred pies for Atherton. She had a home.

Grinning like a giddy fool, she rushed inside and skidded to a stop. Bunk beds nested against one wall, a curtain, pulled back, revealed a small bed and some privacy for her on the opposite side of the cabin, and a table, chairs, dry sink, and a stove filled the rest. Simple but beautiful. Not as big or as nice as the farmhouse they'd left behind, but they would be together, and that alone made it more desirable than a palace.

"Home," she whispered. Jason's shadow filled the doorway and she rounded on him. "It's beautiful, and I am so thankful. This was too kind of you, Jason." Without stopping to think, she rushed up to him and kissed him on the cheek—quite the reach. His eyes widened, then warmed, and she jerked back. "I

—I...thank you." She couldn't find any other words. Maybe he wouldn't read too much into it.

He rubbed his cheek and smiled sideways. "I think it might have been worth it."

———

BY SUNSET, she'd moved in and lit the cookstove. Waiting for the oven to heat up, she wandered out to the porch. Her porch—

She gasped at the sight of a new rocking chair waiting for her.

Jason.

She was going to bake him the best apple pie she'd ever made.

He'd helped her move, brought over some staples, and even chopped some wood before he'd left. But he'd slipped back and deposited this little gift. Harriet ran a hand over the back and then slipped into it. The evening sun was streaming through the pines, streaking the clearing and her porch with long orange and gold fingers. Somewhere in the trees, a whippoorwill heralded the coming night in chorus with the crickets.

She sat back and rocked for a moment, her mind wandering unexpectedly to a dream she'd given up on. Was it still possible? Here, now, at this moment, she had the hope that anything might be possible again. She rose and went inside to her bed. Sifting through a carpet bag, she pulled out her Bible. Not used much, she hid things in it more than she read it.

Her conscience smarting over the thought, she pulled free a postcard and stared at the picture of a lovely, white inn on Mackinac Island in Michigan. Its beautiful columns, red roof, clean lines, and stately presence had, for some reason, always called to her. She could imagine herself the regal lady, running such a lovely hotel, her boys managing the stables and activities for the guests. A silly dream, but she wouldn't be young and able to raise horses her whole life. But a hotel...

She drifted her fingers over the painted card. Yes, she could run a fine hotel with the best kitchen within a thousand miles. She glanced out the small bedroom window. From here, she could just make out some of the details of the bustling, booming Main Street of Blessings. A few buildings, the flowing traffic. Growing. Vibrant. Blessings held promise. Gave her permission to dream again.

She would make it here. Harriet was wiser and older and so much less idealistic. Live and learn, wasn't that the saying? Well, she'd gotten a lifetime of lessons from Henry. Going forward, she would rely on herself. And she would have her ranch and eventually her inn. And no man would figure into the picture again. The rocking chair crossed her mind.

Kind of him, certainly, but her appreciation ended there.

CHAPTER NINE

THE SUN WAS WARM ON JASON'S BACK, BUT EVERYTHING ELSE ON him felt like he'd rolled in a snowbank. The cold of the creek water sinking into his bare toes, he dumped the pan of water and gravel and stood up. The stream was frigid and his back ached ferociously, but he'd collected a few nuggets the size of a fingernail. That would do for the day. If he was going to finish up a few details on this freighting business with Harriet, he'd best get to it. Besides, working on anything that involved the sassy little widow was more interesting than this cold, lonely creek.

He paused and smiled wryly. She was colder than this creek. At least she liked to *pretend* she was frigid as ice water. Jason suspected that was just the hurt talking. Once she healed a little, came to trust him—even the tiniest amount— he expected there'd be some thawing.

Stepping carefully out of the water, he was startled to find Archie Reives watching him from the bank. "Morning, Jason."

"Reives." Jason lifted his hat, shook his sweaty hair dry, and dropped the Stetson back in place. He didn't appreciate being spied on. "Something I can do for you?"

The spindly little man checked his pocket watch, then tucked it back inside his vest pocket. "I heard the cook over at Dundee's place is thinking about opening a freight line."

"Where'd you hear that?"

"Be surprised what you can pick up if you just listen."

Jason wasn't interested. He tossed the pan down and picked up his boots. "This is relevant to me how?"

"Ah, I was just wondering if you knew when she might be ready to open up? She's got horses on the way, I assume. I might have some business for her."

Jason doubted every word coming out of the little praying mantis's mouth. He couldn't say why, but he did. "Well, I'll be sure to mention that to her."

"So, you don't know when she's trying to open?"

Jason tilted his head, openly sharing his suspicious nature. "Why not ask her yourself?"

"Oh, well"—Archie splayed his hands out—"I was passing by, is all. I know you know her. Just thought I'd ask. I want to help her all I can."

"You do, do you?" Jason brushed sand off his right foot and pushed it into his boot. "I'll make sure she knows all about you, Archie."

For just an instant, Archie's brow expressed concern, but he wiped it away with a big grin. "Fine. Fine. And you'll let me know if you hear anything?"

"Certainly." *Not.*

But I'll warn her about you, Archie. I certainly will do that.

Jason had been exceedingly subtle in making inquiries about tack, harnesses, and a barn. Though he couldn't be sure, he guessed he hadn't been subtle enough, and Archie here was the first hint of competition.

STARING into a polished silver tray hanging on the porch post of his little cabin, Jason wet and combed his hair. The reflection lacked clear detail, but his blond hair didn't look too wild. Maybe a touch long. He could use a haircut.

Shrugging, he dropped the comb, grabbed a leather portfolio sitting atop a barrel, and hurried up the main trail to town. He veered off where the pines thinned and headed down toward the river. Harriet's Kitchen, as folks had started calling it, came into sight. Just passing 10:30 in the morning, Jason figured the breakfast rush was gone and she would be between cleaning up and cooking for the noonday meal.

He spotted her just as she snarled and threw a frying pan across a plank table. It took an instant for him to realize her target was Magruder. The man ducked the projectile. Jason launched for the annoying tub of lard just as he bellowed and attempted to scramble clumsily across the table.

Jason caught him and threw him back, slamming him into the other table. A tin can of clean silverware crashed noisily to the ground.

"What's going on here," he demanded, raising his fists at Magruder.

Magruder glared at Harriet then Jason. "I've come for my money Dundee owes me."

"Then get it from him," Harriet shouted, lunging forward. Jason held her back and gave Magruder his own glare.

"Why did she have to throw a frying pan at you, Magruder?"

The implication in the question froze the man. His beady little eyes bugged and he pushed a hand through his sweaty, messy hair. "N—now, Jason, don't go getting the wrong idea. I never laid a hand on her."

"I wasn't going to let you close enough," she snapped and barked like an angry chihuahua.

Again, Jason threw an arm out to keep her from clawing

Magruder's eyes. "Calm down, Harriet. Tell me what happened."

"He came swaggering in here, demanding money, knocking plates and cups to the ground. I didn't know what he intended, so I threw the first thing I found at him."

"If she'da hit me with that thing, she woulda killed me." Magruder straightened up, jutting out his substantial gut. "I'm not the crazy one here." He waved his finger frantically at Harriet. "She's crazy as a badger." He side-stepped away from Jason, attempting to back out of the tent. "But I still want my money."

"Don't come around here anymore, Magruder, if Dundee isn't here. I catch you talking to Mrs. Pullen again, *I'll* throw a frying pan at you...and I won't miss." While Magruder flinched at the promise, Harriet frowned indignantly. Jason waited for the annoying little fat man to run away, then turned to Harriet. "You only missed because you're out of practice."

The stubborn set of her jaw faded...slowly. Finally, she asked, "Why are you here?"

"I wanted to catch you between shifts so I could give you an update." He plucked the portfolio out from under his arm and laid it open on the table. He scanned a page of notes. "Okay, your boys and your horses should arrive in San Francisco on or about June 15th." She gasped, he guessed with excitement, and he smiled. "Cargo includes eight horses, four saddles, various combinations of hitches, harnesses, straps and other tack, and four boxes of replacement parts for the wagons and the tack."

"My boys. My horses. I can't believe it." Harriet sat down beside him. She was beaming, and her smile warmed him like a fire on a cold day. "And replacement parts. I wouldn't have thought of those."

"Something breaks, it'll be hard to get repaired way out here without a pretty lengthy delay."

"You had money for all this?"

"Yes, and it's a good investment. I'm comfortable with what I've spent." He riffled through a few pieces of paper and plucked a ledger page from the stack. "It's all itemized, starting with Nick Sackett heading up to Willamette Valley and rounding up these items."

"Including Whit and Wyatt." She was breathless and her eyes glittered with joy.

"Including Whit and Wyatt. Now"—he pulled another sheet of paper to the top—"this is an agreement with Salazar Patterson. He's got a lean-to and a corral on his parcel. He's going to expand the lean-to into a barn and we'll make it the headquarters for the freight company." He wanted her to see the agreement, that he wasn't hiding anything, and slid it over to her.

Harriet scanned it, absently brushing the tail of her braid back and forth across her palm. A wistful smile hinted that she was seeing the faces of her boys not the words on the page. "June 15th. That's only two weeks."

"About, yes."

She cleared her throat, seemed to ponder something for a moment, then turned to him. "Thank you, Jason. I could have done all this—eventually—but you've certainly made opening a freight company easier and faster. And the faster we're up and running, the faster I'll have a ranch again."

Jason wondered if he'd heard a little tiny crack in all that ice around Harriet's heart. "I'm glad you were smart enough to let me help." He started gathering up the papers when he thought of something. "By the way, if you run into a man named Archie Reives, remember one thing: he is not your friend, and he may even be your competition."

"Competition?"

"Just a suspicion I have, but he runs a boat up and down the river, delivering supplies, miners, whatever anybody needs. I wouldn't doubt he's got his eye on land routes."

"How will I know him?"

Jason stood and she followed him, curious for the answer. "He's a gangly fella, and there's something...*insect*-like about him. He always makes me think of a hungry praying mantis."

Harriet shivered. She hated bugs. "At least you didn't say cockroach."

He tucked the portfolio under his arm. "Don't see much difference."

CHAPTER TEN

"You can't quit!" Dundee positively shrieked. He raked his fingers through his hair and left the graying mass in complete disarray. "You're the best cook I've ever had."

Harriet shoved a pie into the oven, shut the door, and faced her employer. "I'll work another couple of weeks, Dundee, but I came to Blessings so I could gather my family and rebuild a dream." She realized her stance was tense and lowered her shoulders. "I'm sorry. You gave me employment when I needed it. I'll try to find someone to take over for me, but the moment my boys are here with the horses, I'm in a different profession."

Several emotions battled across the man's face, from consternation to vexation, but acceptance finally won. "Well, I reckon that's all I can expect. I will miss your pies, Mrs. Pullen."

"Now, why would you be giving up on your pies, Mrs. Pullen?"

A tall, skinny man in a checked suit sidled up to them. Harriet knew him right away, based on Jason's description.

Archie Reives. And Jason had warned her not to give anything away.

"I was thinking of trying another pastry," she said, praying Dundee would go along. "Turnovers possibly."

"Funny," the bug of a man said. "I heard you were thinking of opening a shipping company."

Dundee's eyes widened, but only because Harriet had told him she was trying to keep this hush-hush until her horses arrived. Harriet, for her part, opted not to take the bait. "I'm sorry, you are...?"

"Reives." He extended his long arm for a handshake. "Archie Reives." The two shook. "I am only curious about the possibility as it would be such an unusual and, dare I say, dangerous venture for a woman to attempt. Don't you think, Dundee?"

Dundee blinked his shock away and narrowed his eyes at Mr. Reives. "This gal, mate, can do anything she darn well puts her mind to. I know. I've seen how much sand she's got." A righteous indignation seemed to rise in him and he poked Mr. Reives in the chest. "If she opens a freight line or a bakery or a hat shop, you'd best not stand in her way. A donk like you won't even slow her down."

Mr. Reives frowned at the poke and inched back, but then a cold, thin smile painted over the annoyance. "I didn't mean to offend her or you, Dundee. Just trying to pass along some neighborly advice." He shifted back to Harriet. "You've gotta worry about more than the elements and the terrain. The most dangerous animal out here is man."

Harriet considered the meaning behind the statement. A veiled threat? "You run a river freight business, isn't that correct, Mr. Reives?"

"Yes, ma'am."

"You're not worried about a little competition, are you?"

He chuckled. "From a woman? No offense, but no, I'm not

worried about a little competition from you or anybody else. As a matter of fact, I *am* branching out to land routes. I've got a fine shipment of horses coming up from Texas. Solid and strong. I'll move freight through these mountains so fast I'll leave your pretty little head spinning."

Harriet held her face still but she was alarmed to hear Reives already had horses on the way. Of course, hers were much closer than Texas, but when had his animals shipped? "When are you opening?"

He grinned, and this time, the smile was honest. "As soon as I can."

————

HARRIET TRIED to ignore how warm and comforting Jason felt pressed up against her. He had his hands over her eyes and was sort of pushing and leading her toward something. He loved these little surprises.

She could hear the river, but it was a ways away. The scent of pine filled the air, and she thought she heard the faint jingle of wagons and men muttering in the distance. So they were just outside Blessings but not too terribly far from the river?

"Just a few more steps," he said.

For a moment longer, Harriet let her anger and defensiveness rest and enjoyed the tickle of Jason's breath in her ear, the goosebumps rising on her from his body heat. She rationalized that he affected her this way because it had been so long since *any* man—particularly a sober one—had touched her. She wouldn't allow the possibility there was anything special about the man holding her now.

"All right, ready?"

Harriet nodded.

Jason chuckled softly and pulled his hands away. Harriet

blinked, clearing her vision, to see a barn. Salazar's lean-to, but greatly expanded into a full-size barn.

"Your office, so to speak."

"The barn. Our barn." *Our barn?* Why had she said that? Well, she meant...well, he *was* a partner. And her sons were coming. It was *our barn.* Oh, she was pleased. "It's fine, Jason, more than fine. We need my boys and those horses to hurry up and get here."

"We'll beat Reives. Don't worry."

Harriet wasn't sure she'd know how to act when she saw Whit and Wyatt again. She thought she might embarrass them. Not on purpose, but she was going to hug and kiss them like she hadn't seen them in years, not a few months. Getting her freight line up and running before that scalawag Reives was just icing on the cake.

"Have you been able to determine when his horses might get to Blessings?"

Jason hooked his thumbs on his belt loops. "I hear they might be here in a couple of weeks."

Harriet released a soft whistle. "That's a little too close."

"Maybe, but we'll—"

Approaching hoofbeats cut off his words. He and Harriet turned to see a rider bursting out of the woods. Fear gripped her heart. Something was wrong, she could feel it in her soul.

Jason took a step forward and waved the rider in. Harriet recognized Dundee quickly and stepped up beside Jason as the man reined in. He was pale, breathing hard, and wore a mask of grief. Unusually nimble, perhaps because his news outweighed his aches and pains, he swung from the saddle and gripped Harriet's hands. "I'm sorry, girl. Word has just come up from the coast. The ship carrying your boys—oh, Harriet, I'm so sorry. It went down in a storm."

CHAPTER ELEVEN

THE BLOOD DRAINED FROM HARRIET'S BRAIN. SHE LOST THE feeling in her legs and started to fall, but Jason caught her. Surely she hadn't heard correctly. It couldn't be true...

"Are you sure?" Jason asked, his voice tight and strangled.

"That's the word. The Sea Witch went down in a storm only a few miles from the San Francisco Bay."

"N-no survivors?" Harriet couldn't believe it. Whit and Wyatt *had* to be fine. This information was wrong. They were both strong swimmers.

"No teenage boys," Dundee said huskily, "no horses in the...wreckage." He swallowed. "Presumed lost at sea. I'm sorry." He snatched off his glasses and wiped at his eyes.

Harriet's brain froze over with a sudden chill. She couldn't fathom these words, their meaning. None of this made any sense to her. Whit and Wyatt couldn't be...dead?

"When?" Jason held her tighter. "When did the ship sink?"

Sink?

"Little over a week ago." Dundee shook his head and turned to his horse. "Again, I'm so sorry." Slowly, wearily, his energy gone, he replaced his glasses and dragged himself into the saddle. "Please, if you need anything—" His voice broke and he clamped his mouth shut.

"Thank you," Jason said, pulling Harriet tighter to his side. Dundee nodded and rode off as Jason wrapped Harriet in a tight embrace. "Harriet—"

"Ships don't sink. They float." The vivid image of a ship flailing in rough water, her sons being tossed about in rough seas, the horses screaming and splashing in panic brutally drove home the news. Her heart split in two with raging grief and she wailed into Jason's chest. "No, no, no..."

Jason squeezed her tighter. "Shhhh." Unfathomable agony exploded in her, ripping sobs from her. She writhed in anguish, wailing, sobbing, and he held her tighter still. "Harriet, I'm so, so sorry."

The grief in his own voice, choking it, breaking it, took all of Harriet's strength. She fell against him and wept with an agony that flowed from her core like hot, seething lava.

———

JASON QUIETLY WATCHED Harriet going through the motions of baking a pie. He couldn't imagine what drove her on. She had taken two days to hide in her cabin, grieving her children as word of her loss flooded Blessings. Miners, prospectors, shop owners and their families drifted by, offering sincere but awkward condolences, hugs, and food. Jason had stood by her side for much of it, but he suspected she didn't even realize it, her grief was so blinding.

Now, as she grimly rolled out the dough for a pie, he guessed it may well have been the generous but abysmal food that drove her back to the kitchen. Also, he knew she found solace in baking.

He wished he had some pressure gauge like that. He missed those two boys and couldn't vent his grief in such a tangible way. He'd gone riding this morning to a remote spot. There, he'd released an anguished yell and emptied his gun into the air. Then he'd listened to the echo roll across the valley of pines and rocks. A release of sorts, it had helped, but only in a very small way.

Then, to hear Reives's horses would arrive in Blessings in about a week—maddening. Salt in the wound. Harriet's animals would have beat his here, giving her and Jason a fine head start on the freight line. Hard as it was, though, Jason knew all of this was in the palm of God's hands. Nothing surprised Him. He had a plan, and it would unfurl as it was supposed to.

Sighing, he slipped beneath the tent and snatched his hat off. "Harriet?" She started but didn't turn around. He heard sniffles, realized she was wiping her eyes frantically. "Maybe it's too soon to be back in the kitchen."

She straightened and rounded slowly on him. "It's never too soon for that." They both smiled awkwardly at the weak joke, and she took a few steps toward him, her chin quivering.

Despite her red-rimmed eyes, she was such a pretty thing. How many times back in Sundown had he daydreamed of loosening that braid of hers, running his hands through all the silky gold strands, claiming that sassy mouth? Now, he just wanted to hold and comfort her.

"You're probably here about the money you fronted—"

"Money?" Jason was literally aghast. "You think I'm here about money?"

She stuttered for a moment. "W—well, I just assumed because of all the money you spent for the freight—"

"Hang the money." Dang if she couldn't be an aggravating woman sometimes. Did she really think that lowly of him? "I came to check on *you*. I know how bad I miss Whit and Wyatt. I can't imagine what you're going through."

She seemed taken aback by his indignation. Her eyes

widened and her lips trembled. "I'm sorry. I know you were fond of them." Suddenly she deflated like a good wind leaving a ship's sails and dropped down at a table. "You're right. You can't imagine. I've lost everything, Jason. I've never been so alone, so empty, and so furious with God before." She hid her face in her hands. "The hurt is indescribable. My boys..." she trailed off in a hoarse whisper.

He settled beside her and raised an arm to hug her. She leaned into him and wept. He marveled over the feel of her tears soaking through his shirt. He ached for her and if he'd had the power, would have taken this grief onto himself.

Instead, all he could offer was an embrace and overused words. "I'm sorry, Harriet. So sorry."

A shuffling noise drew his eyes up. He was surprised to see Atherton Winslet striding toward them, his hat tucked respectfully at his chest, gray hair dancing in the morning breeze. Jason hadn't ever seen the old gentleman move so fast or nimbly.

"News," the old man called, his aged face glowing with it. "I have good news!" Harriet and Jason rose to meet him. He raced up and clutched her shoulders. "God giveth and He taketh away. There's a string of horses coming into town." His gaze shot to Jason. "Nick Sackett is at the lead..." He returned to Harriet. "And, God be praised, two young boys are bringing up the rear!"

———

Joy—so pure and exquisite it left Harriet breathless—coursed through her. Whit and Wyatt were riding two sorrels hell-bent for leather down Blessings Main Street. Word had spread about the impending arrival, and it looked to her like most of the town was here, waving and cheering.

From the saddle of his own horse, Jason greeted the thundering herd at the intersection of Main and First and waved for them to follow him. Harriet shouted and screamed with schoolgirl giddiness at Whit and Wyatt as they rode by, tipping their hats. A little gaunt, a touch pale, but smiles lit up their faces.

"We made it, Ma!" Whit yelled, waving his hat in the air, his horse moving at a full gallop.

"We sure as heck did," Wyatt added, thundering after his brother.

Harriet gathered her skirt and took off down the muddy street at a full run, intent on smothering her two boys—no, her two *young men*—with hugs and kisses when they dismounted at the corral.

She was winded when the corral and all the bustling, prancing horses came into view. Revived by joy, she raced the rest of the way, flinging herself onto Whit and Wyatt as they stood holding their mounts. Squeals of delight and good-natured laughter erupted as they hugged each other.

Harriet could have died of pure happiness at that moment. She had her sons back from the dead. "Thank You, thank You, thank You," she repeated to God while peppering frantic kisses on her boys' faces. She finished with one long, breath-stealing hug.

A large crowd of curious townsfolk had followed them out to the new office. Reggie Wallace took advantage of the calm moment to shake the boys' hands. "Gentlemen, I heard about your epic ride." Harriet was puzzled by this statement as Reggie slapped Whit on the shoulder. "I feel confident my items will make it through with drivers like you. Let me know when you're open for business."

"Yes, sir," Whit said, his perpetually red cheeks blazing now. "Will do."

Harriet waited for Reggie to get out of earshot before she closed in. "What does he mean epic adventure?"

A tall, thin man with stringy, dark hair and a patch over one eye stepped up, tapping his thigh with his hat. "It's no small thing what your boys did, Mrs. Pullen." Harriet smiled. Jason had told her about Nick Sackett. "Swimming horses out of an angry ocean, ridin' 'em a hundred miles—bareback—on dangerous, unfamiliar terrain, and followin' a one-eyed Indian for a guide. A straight-up miracle."

"Mr. Sackett." She clutched his hand, almost choking up again with emotion. "You brought me my boys, safe and sound. I don't care what you call it. And I can't thank you enough."

He shrugged, embarrassed by her gushing. "We're here because we all worked together."

Harriet exhaled a deep, joyful breath and squeezed her boys' cheeks—to their horror. She laughed, delirious with joy.

"You know," Jason said from behind her, "we've only beat Reives by about three or four days."

Harriet clutched Whit's and Wyatt's hands. "It'll be enough. He's never gone up against us."

CHAPTER TWELVE

JASON ALMOST COULDN'T BELIEVE WHAT HE WAS HEARING. HE swallowed his last sip of beer and paused the empty mug at his lips, listening intently to the load of horse manure Archie Reives was dumping two tables over.

"A woman can't run a business like a freight line. It's just too dangerous. Too arduous."

Jason's eyes met Ellie's, the short, plump owner of the saloon whose outrageous red hair had made her something of a celebrity in town. "Every time he opens his mouth," she said quietly, "he proves what a fool he is." Jason chuckled at the observation.

Ben and Reuben Baird, two guards from the mine, nodded in agreement with Reives. "We've got our hands full as it is at the mine," Reuben, a broad, stocky fella, was saying. "I can't imagine how a woman is gonna stand up to rowdies everywhere else."

"Especially a little thing like her," Ben added.

"She should stick to baking pies." That was Lucas Barfield from the leather shop. "Maybe she thinks she's a man. Next thing we know, she'll be wearing pants."

"Pants or not," Archie continued, "she doesn't know diddly squat about horses."

Jason slammed his mug down. The men at the table cut their eyes at him. Hands clenching into fists, he turned to face Archie squarely. "And you're a rabble-rousing, lying lickspittle." Silence, somber as a graveyard at midnight, fell on the saloon. Men watched with wary eyes. Jason took a few steps toward the table. "Harriet Pullen raised some of the finest horses in the territory up at her ranch in the Willamette Valley. She rides better than most men I know. Her horses are so well-trained they do tricks for her." He let his searing gaze graze slowly over each man at the table. "When you can say the same, then run your mouths."

Archie placed his cards facedown and rose to his feet. "She opens this business, the men of this town are just going to wind up retrieving her body and dead horses from beside the trail."

"She's not doing this alone, Reives." Jason raised his hand and pointed his index finger at the man. "You keep that in mind." A few years in law enforcement had taught him to walk away from pointless arguments, but right now, he wanted to throttle Archie Reives so bad he could taste it. "You're just afraid of the competition. And you know what?"

"What?"

"You should be." Jason had put his money on Harriet and her horses for a reason. "Your Texas horses will be eating her dust." His point made and the desire for any more beer snuffed by the saloon's current clientele, Jason stormed out.

"No woman should run a business like this," Reives called after him. "If you were a man and not her lapdog, you'd see that!"

———

JASON SAT on the front porch of his simple one-room cabin, chair leaned back, feet resting on the rail. He closed his eyes and listened to the bubbling laughter from the creek forty or so feet down from him.

If you were a man and not her lapdog, you'd see that!

His eyes flew open. The accusation was patently untrue, but it still made him want to pummel Reives. Harriet would have to know Jason was alive to first delegate him to lapdog.

"Jason, mate," a voice hailed from the darkness.

Startled at first, Jason dropped his feet and his chair and stood, peering into the shadows, made starker by the brilliant moon. But he knew that Australian accent. "Willoughby?"

"Aye."

Jason waited for the man to break free from the trees before he spoke again. "What are you doing out here?"

"Came to see you." The trader approached and stopped at the bottom step, resting one foot on it.

Willoughby had never come to see Jason before, and he was immediately suspicious of this visit. "What can I do for you?"

A slight moon cast enough light on the man's round face to show a shadow on his brow. He shoved his hands in his pockets and shrugged his shoulders. "Some of the merchants asked me to speak with ya about Mrs. Pullen's freight service. We think you should talk her out of it."

Offended, though he wasn't quite sure by what, Jason crossed his arms over his chest. "Reives send you to see me?"

"No, but he's been doin' most of the talkin'. Listen, Jason, word is the lady is going to drive her own wagons. Now, I don't like Reives, and I see the game he's playing, but it's true the profession is too dangerous for a woman."

Jason scratched his chin, trying to pinpoint why this conversation grated on his nerves. Turned out to be a couple of things. "First of all, you and the other men in Blessings aren't some kind of arbiters of who can open what kind of business in town. You start with Harriet, who's next? Second of all, she *is* capable of running this business and driving her own wagons. Honestly, it kinda makes me a little angry that you and Reives and whoever else are sitting on your high horses telling her what she can and can't do, much less with her own property."

"Well, it's not like that exactly—"

"No, that's exactly what it's like." He dropped his hands to his hips. "Tell Reives I won't be talking to Harriet about shutting down. Tell him the only way to get her out of the business is to beat her fair and square."

CHAPTER THIRTEEN

IN THE MERCANTILE, HARRIET PERUSED A SHELF STOCKED WITH a decent selection of canned fruit. She missed cooking for her boys and was enjoying the few meals they'd had together, but she could do better than rabbit stew and apple pie.

She heard her name and stopped to eavesdrop on two men discussing her over the pickle barrel. "Ah, I don't know what she's thinking. Reives has a point. Who's gonna risk sending a shipment of anything valuable over the mountains with a *woman?*"

"Yeah." The other man chuckled. "Mighty full of herself, I think."

Harriet bit down hard to keep from screaming. No, not the whole town of Blessings thought a woman couldn't run a freight business, but what if enough did that more business went to Reives than her?

She'd lose everything...again. Because of men and their selfish, petty jealousies. Well, she was here. Her boys were here. And her horses were here.

If Archie Reives thought he was going to gossip enough to

shut her down with rumors and ignorance, he most certainly had another think coming.

———

JASON PLACED the plank atop the two barrels and stepped back. No, it wasn't much of a desk. He glanced around the little room that they'd added on to the barn and allowed a wry grin. Spartan, simple—one window for light, a buck stove against the outer wall, a makeshift desk, and a stool for a chair —but it was their office, and he was more than a little proud. He was eager for Harriet to see it.

Speaking of—

He checked his pocket watch. Ten after eight. She was late. He peered out the window. Whit and Wyatt were hitching a bay gelding up to the buckboard for some training. The ship-wreck had deprived the company of two new wagons, but Jason had managed to do a little horse-trading and round up this buckboard and one Conestoga. It was a start.

He drummed his fingers on his thighs. Should he worry? *Lord, just how underhanded might Archie Reives get besides stirring up merchants against Harriet?*

She walked into sight just then, her head high, her gait brisk, a basket swinging on her arm. She smiled and waved at her boys and Jason's heart did a funny kind of flutter. He liked the way her face lit with joy at the sight of her children, the way the morning sun glinted off the top of her head, like she created her own glow. And even though that brown muslin dress had seen better days, it fit her nicely. She'd never be confused for a man, in pants or not.

He opened the door and watched her hug her boys, much to their embarrassment. They pulled away from her and glanced around to make sure no one had seen the syrupy affection. Jason knew more and more every day what he wanted out of Blessings, and gold had very little to do with it.

"Make sure you don't get that tug buckle too tight," Harriet said, leaving them. "And work on backing up." She saw Jason and raised the basket. "But first, apple fritters for breakfast."

Jason licked his lips. He loved Harriet's apple fritters. "That makes my day."

"Good." She turned back to Whit and Wyatt. "Boys, come get a fritter and give me a minute. I have something to tell everyone."

CHAPTER FOURTEEN

JASON STOOD BESIDE HARRIET AS SHE EMPTIED THE CONTENTS of the basket on the desk. Fresh, warm apple fritters wrapped in brown paper. The scents of sugar and cinnamon, mixed with something uniquely Harriet, turned his knees to water. The more he was around her, the more often that happened—

The thought stopped his hand as he reached for a fritter. For the first time, he realized that might not be such a good thing. What if winning her wasn't God's will? What if his feelings for Harriet were never returned?

"What's the matter?" Harriet eyed the fritter. "Did you see a bug or something?"

"No, I..." He picked up the pastry. "Nothing. Just had a stray thought." The boys clattered in and stormed toward the desk, bumping, bustling, trying to block each other in case there wasn't enough to go around.

"Boys," Harriet scolded. "Act like you've got some manners. There's plenty."

Jason moved over a little and grinned as Wyatt, the younger but stockier son, tried elbowing the taller and ganglier Whit out of the way. They succeeded in getting to the desk simultaneously and earning a thunderous look from Harriet for the rough-housing.

"And take off your hats." The boys immediately obeyed, snatching them off and crushing the cowboy hats beneath their arms.

"What's your news?" Jason asked quickly, trying to get them out of hot water.

Harriet took a deep breath and eyed the three of them for a moment. "I talked Mr. Winslet into sponsoring a contest. If we win, we get all his shipping business."

Whit slowed the fritter on the way to his mouth. "That's a good thing, right?"

"He founded the town. Owns almost everything here."

"He'd be the largest customer," Jason added, but something about this idea bothered him. "What happens if we lose? And who's in this contest with us? Reives? Exactly how do you see it working?"

"We're going to take a shipment for him from Blessings to Truckee and back. Whoever does it the fastest wins."

"Have you laid out rules, limitations, routes?"

Harriet's face fell. "W-well, no. Not yet. I didn't get that specific. We've got to put all that together."

Now Jason could pinpoint what sat wrong here. She hadn't discussed it with him. Not even a hint. It rankled him. He supposed it was her business—no, it wasn't, he corrected himself. Weren't they partners? She couldn't go off half-cocked. He had some knowledge to add to the mix, some rights to protect. *And it's not my ego talking, Lord. I have wise counsel to offer. Make her listen.* "Yeah. We have to talk about it."

———

HARRIET DIDN'T MISS the impatient tone in Jason's voice. She wondered what she'd done to annoy him, but wasn't going to play any games finding out. "Boys, why don't you go on and finish those fritters outside? Get back to training that horse."

"Okay, sure."

"Yes, ma'am."

Juggling hats and fritters, Whit and Wyatt went back to work and Harriet dove into the matter at hand. "What's wrong?"

Jason pulled a pinch from his fritter, chewed it slowly, then licked his lips. "Am I your partner?"

"You are my partner."

"Then don't you think you should have talked to me about this contest?"

"I am talking to you about it."

"*Before* you went to Atherton."

Harriet folded her arms, trying to squelch her anger. All she could think about was how many times Henry had injected his two cents into her decisions. He had just wanted control. He'd never cared about the ranch, how to invest in its future. Only getting down to the bottom dollar as fast as possible, by any means. She opened her mouth to set Jason straight on a few things when he tossed up a hand.

"Don't say anything you're going to regret, Harriet. I can see you're mad."

"You're dang straight I'm mad. Yes, you put some money into this venture. Yes, you're taking a risk on me, but this is *my* company." She slapped her chest with each point. "They're *my* horses. *I* gave up my boys to come here alone. I will make this freight company successful because I'm going to pour every ounce of blood, sweat, and tears I have into it. Money doesn't buy that kind of investment."

Harriet knew she'd gone too far, but better Jason understood where things stood now rather than later. His expression seemed to harden, as if his skin were made of glass. "And pure, blind ambition," he said the word as if it repulsed him, "born of hate or revenge—or even fear—won't make the company successful either, Harriet."

She felt as if he'd slapped her. The words stung because they had pierced to the heart of why she was doing this. His keen observation was an unexpected intimacy between them she wouldn't have allowed, given a choice. Then again, what did it matter? She had never meant to hide her ambition, and the reasons behind it *were* patently clear.

"Ambition, Jason, can only help. The motivation doesn't matter."

Gazes locked on one another, tension heavy as an October snow fell over them. Harriet resented the disappointment in his eyes. He had no right to judge her.

Finally, Jason set the remainder of his fritter back down on the brown paper. "Seem to have lost my appetite, but thank you."

Without another word or a glance her way, he swiped his hat off the desk and trudged from their office.

———

A LOT of places a man could go to think, but Jason wound up on a bench in front of the mercantile. Sitting quietly, watching the traffic flow by. He wouldn't lose his temper here. He wouldn't hear Harriet hammering on this idea of ambition, justifying her selfishness. He wouldn't hear Archie Reives's snide *lapdog* reference here. No, he'd enjoy the morning's summer warmth, find some calm in the scents of green grass, horse manure, and baking bread drifting to him.

Until he realized his right hand kept clenching into a fist. He drifted for a moment with the idea of laying Harriet Pullen across his knee and paddling her rear end. He understood she'd been hurt, but she was letting the tragedy change her into a creature blinded by ambition and fueled by hate. Something needed to knock some sense into her.

He hoped it wouldn't be a tragedy. They weren't exactly few and far between in boomtowns, much less in the freighting industry. Too many things could go wrong. The woman had no idea.

He would have thought nearly losing Whit and Wyatt would have humbled her some. Instead, the tragedy that wasn't had only added fuel to her fire. Her way or no way. Jason had never seen the beat—

A squeal—no, a scream of rage—brought him back to the moment, and he tracked the sound. Down the boardwalk aways, he spotted three men surrounding something or someone. They were throwing their heads back and laughing. One was waving a pair of pants over his head. Peering closer, Jason saw between their shoulders a hand—a feminine hand—grabbing for the pants.

Righteous fury boiled his blood. Jason surged to his feet and rushed down the walk.

"Give me those back," the woman yelled.

He stumbled, almost stopped. Harriet? That was Harriet's voice. Alarmed now, he reached the scuffle in three long steps and grabbed one of the thugs by the neck. Short, slovenly, smelling like cow dung, he was several inches shorter than Jason. He clawed at the hand on his neck, but Jason handily slung him away from the tiff. The man went flying, landing in the dirt with a loud thud. The melee ended abruptly as the other two, just as smelly and unkempt, each took a step back. Harriet snatched a pair of dungarees from one of them and retreated behind Jason.

"What's going on here, boys," he asked, eyeing them warily, especially the one staggering up from the ground.

"Breeches," Harriet spat. "They tried to steal my package and the dungarees fell out. They started asking me if I was going to wear them." She leaned forward. So mad spittle was flying from her mouth, she pointed at the man on the ground. "He—he asked me vulgar questions about—things."

Jason passed a restraining hand in front of her. "Calm down, Harriet."

"Don't tell me to calm down."

Momentarily distracted by her snap at him, Jason nearly missed the man on the ground lunging to his feet and throwing an uppercut. Jason avoided it but felt the breeze. And smelled the liquor. In the same instant, he shoved Harriet back and hit the man with a powerful jab to the nose.

Cartilage crunched and the man howled. Clutching his face, he dropped to his knees once again. His buddies inched a little further back.

Fixing to bolt. "Aah, aah, aah, boys." Jason waved a finger at them. "Nobody is going anywhere until Mrs. Pullen here tells me what she'd like to do with you."

"We weren't doing nothin'," the fella with the bleeding nose protested. "Just having a little fun is all." He snatched a bandana from his back pocket and pressed it to his bloody face. "We heard how bossy she is and how she thinks she can drive a freight wagon like a man."

"I never said that," Harriet yelled, lunging at the men, but Jason grabbed her. Face flushed, lips tight, she squirmed and fussed in his arms like a rabid fox. Dang if she wasn't hell-bent on a fight with somebody in this town.

She reminded Jason of a raccoon he'd tangled with once. The animal nearly killed him. Took three rounds with an axe handle to put it down. For a few minutes of the fight, it was touch and go.

"It's all anybody's talking about," one of the other men chimed in to defend their actions. A burning glare from Harriet and Jason had him hunkering down like a beat dog.

She lunged again, but Jason held firm. "Calm down,

Harriet. Calm down." Finally, she settled…a little. "All right…
Well…" Jason loosened his grip a little. Trusting she had
regained some sense, he let her go. "Want me to take them to
Pete? Let them spend the night in jail. You can press charges."

Harriet clutched the breeches tighter, twisting and stran-
gling them. "No." She wilted a little. "No, release them. I don't
want to see them again."

Jason debated the wisdom of releasing the hooligans but
figured he'd better agree for the moment. "You heard the lady.
Get out of here and don't make me regret letting this pass."
Because he would have preferred giving them a sound thrash-
ing. It angered him greatly they thought they could treat a
woman, especially Harriet, like that. They waved Jason off like
he was a troublesome fly and slogged down the boardwalk.

He huffed a deep, exasperated breath but didn't look at the
feisty little critter beside him. "You all right?"

"I'm fine."

He watched the troublesome fellas for another minute
then shook his head. "Reives is running his mouth, Harriet.
Telling everybody who will listen you can't run a business.
You're a strong-willed, foolish woman who doesn't know her
place."

"Is he saying that, or are you?"

Jason re-situated his hat, jarred askew by the encounter.
"Not me. I think you can do it. But you'll have to prove yourself to the town." And get that temper under control.

"I thought the contest might do that for me."

He cut his eyes over at her. "Us." His frustration with
Harriet returning, he faced her, crossing his arms over his
chest as if he was about to scold a child. "It's not about who
has put in more money or even why you're doing this. The
fact is we're all in this together now, Harriet. You, me, and
your boys. What will make your freight company successful is
if we all work together."

She raised her nose in the air and folded her arms. As adorable as she was, all huffy and flushed, mussed up braid shimmering on her shoulder, he still felt like wringing her neck. Tempted to walk away—*sorely* tempted—he stared at her, trying to burn some sense into her head.

After a moment, she softened. A little. "You're right. We have to be a team." She glanced down the walk. "I think we should go see Reives and discuss the contest. The both of us. Together."

Jason ran his tongue over his teeth, questioning her contriteness and pondering the suggestion. Word was no doubt already circulating about the contest. No backing out now. "*Fine.* We will go talk to him."

CHAPTER FIFTEEN

Harriet was absolutely livid over having so much of her fate fall again into the hands of men. Striding down the boardwalk, Jason beside her, she was at once both furious with him...and grateful for him. He'd stopped the shenanigans with those three slackers, but then he'd talked to her as if she were a child. She irrationally entertained the idea of throwing something at him.

Calm down. Calm down, he said. HE can calm down. He wasn't the one getting accosted on the street. And he wants to talk to me like I'm five. "Fine, we will go talk to him." Like I needed his permission to talk to this Reives—

"You're muttering, Harriet."

"I am not." But, of course, she was. She clamped her jaws.

"Have you always been this hot-tempered?"

She tried to think. Once upon a time, she and Henry had worked side-by-side building their home, then the corrals. Then the boys had come along...and he had started drinking more, staying out later and later, disappearing in the middle of chores. By the time Whit was five, Henry was rarely home, and when he was, he was more of a disruption to their routine than a part of it. Foolishly, she had fought for her husband's attention by throwing kitchen pans at him. The tantrums, however, had only gained her an undesirable reputation as a shrew.

Realizing the harm her outbursts did to her children and her reputation, Harriet had reigned in her temper. "Truth be told, I haven't thrown anything in years."

"Bringing something under control is different from keeping it on a slow boil."

"You think I'm an explosion waiting to happen?"

He sucked on his teeth for a second. "You were ready to tear those fellas back there limb from limb. You should have seen your face."

"I had every right to be furious with those men."

"Yeah, I suppose."

"What?" Aghast, Harriet stopped and grabbed Jason's elbow, forcing him to face her. "*They* accosted *me*."

Towering over her, he rested his hands on his hips and scoured her face. His blue eyes bore into her, but she was too mad to care how handsome he was. She wanted him to stop making these cryptic references.

Finally, he let out a long, slow breath. "I think you're so mad at your husband for causing all this you could spit nails."

"Of course I am."

Jason swiped a hand over his mouth, dragged it along his jaw, and finished with a squeeze to his neck muscles. "You are a pain. You're letting all that anger blind you to—" He seemed to ponder the next words carefully. "Wise, deliberate actions. Like this contest with Reives. We should have talked about it. Instead, you went off half-cocked—"

"I'm not going over this ground again. I said you were right and I would involve you in future decisions. I'll play on our team, but you"—she grit her teeth together and poked him in the chest—"have to stop treating me like a child."

Jason's eyes widened, and he straightened up a little. "I didn't realize I was."

"I may be angry. I may be a little headstrong. I should've included you in the discussion about the contest, but I'm in a hurry, Jason. I don't have time to pretend I'm at a tea party. I'm building a business, a future for myself and my children. I'll try to include you if you'll quit dragging your feet."

And that was all the compromise Harriet was in the mood for.

Jason considered things for a moment, then finally nodded. "All right. Let's get this over with."

———

IT TOOK A LITTLE TRACKING, but Harriet and Jason found Archie Reives down at his dock. He'd had one built for his own boat and wouldn't be sharing it with Dundee, or so Harriet had heard. Undaunted by the less-than-cooperative attitude of the man, Dundee had built his wharf roughly a hundred feet down from Reives. It was one hundred yards long and paralleled the clear, jade, western bank of the American River. Reives's dock jutted out into the water and was only slightly longer than his hundred-foot paddle-wheeler. A sizable boat, peeling paint, rotten decking, and rusty metal marred what could have been an otherwise impressive vessel.

"I think he made a mistake," Harriet said, eyeing the wharf. "Dundee is going to have a big operation."

"I don't think Reives ever had any intention of making the river his main source of income. Look at the boat." Jason clutched Harriet's elbow as they navigated the swaying dock. "No, he's more interested in running crooked card games and getting his own overland freight business up."

"Jason, Mrs. Pullen." Reives was coming down the side staircase of the boat and waved them aboard. "Step on." He met them at the bottom and shook Jason's hand, then appreciatively surveyed Harriet. "I have heard so much about you, Mrs. Pullen."

"Don't you mean you've *talked* so much about me?"

A slender man in a cheap suit, the fake smile slid off his face. "I'm sure I don't know what you mean."

"I'm sure you don't."

"Listen, Archie," Jason intervened, "we've come about a little business. Harriet here has a proposition for ya."

The fake smile returned, but the truth glittered in his beady little eyes. "What can I do for you?"

"Mr. Winslet has agreed to let us compete for his business. The winner gets all his shipping."

Reives's eyebrows rose and he hung a bony hand on the small pocket of his vest. "Really, now? *All* his business?"

"All. You and I just need to come up with a fair competition. Rules and such."

Reives's curious gaze ricocheted back and forth between Harriet and Jason. "Is this on the level, Jason? I beat her and get all of Winslet's shipping in and out of Blessings?"

"You have to beat her. That's the hard part."

Reives chuckled, soft and low at first, then he turned away, laughing outright. "Oh, this is..." He didn't finish, seemed to ponder things a moment, then wheeled on them. "I'm all for this. Let's talk details."

"Well, I—I thought we might keep it simple. Race from here to Truckee and back. First one home wins."

"Rules?" Reives asked.

"None. You find the best, fastest route."

"Wait a minute, wait a minute." Jason waved a hand between them. "I'm not good with that, Harriet. We need rules. Otherwise Reives here will drive straight through someone's front room to beat us."

"Who says *I* wouldn't do that?" Jason's face hardened at her answer, but she ignored him and rushed on. "The only requirement is the freight is delivered in good condition."

"And who decides that?" Reives asked immediately.

"Mr. Winslet."

Reives worked his jaw back and forth. "Restrictions on team changes, drivers, route choices, wagons, anything?"

"None." Oh, she could feel the heat coming off Jason in waves. "Jason, do you have a problem with any of this?"

"Nice of you to ask." He turned more to Archie. "There should be an official start/finish line. And we should limit the wagon to one Conestoga of equal weight. We'll have an official weigh-in before the start. At least two team changes. That's to prevent you from driving your horses into the ground."

Reives slid his tongue over his bottom lip while he again eyed Harriet. "All right." He thrust out a hand to her, his sleeve sliding up and revealing a thin, frail-looking wrist. "I can live with those rules, except my horses are still on the way from Texas. They should be here any day, but they'll need time to recover."

"Two weeks." She reached for his hand but stopped just short of shaking it. He considered the suggestion and nodded. Harriet sealed the agreement with a firm grip. "I'm going to win, Mr. Reives."

"I've no doubt you'll try, Mrs. Pullen."

CHAPTER SIXTEEN

Now Jason could spit nails. He waited till they were out of sight of Reives's boat and in a cluster of pines before he grabbed Harriet's shoulder and jerked her to a stop. "Do you have any idea what you've done?" She glared at his hand and then him. Immediately, he regretted his gruffness and unhanded her. "I'm sorry." Surprised at the emotions she loosed in him, he dropped his fist to his side. "But you just gave a professional con man the legal right to cheat in this contest."

"And you have no faith in my horses. It doesn't matter if he cheats. We'll still beat him. We can take the shortest route, no matter how steep. From here to Truckee, we should only need to switch horses once, but we can go twice now. What do you mean con man?"

"I know Reives from some wanted posters. He runs what are called confidence games. He sets up elaborate plays and swindles folks out of their money. But he'll cheat just to avoid playing by the rules. It's in his blood."

"I still say it doesn't matter. We'll watch him. Closely."

God, Jason prayed beyond frustrated, *please give this woman some wisdom. Or at least humility.* "I guess we will."

––––––

JASON HAD MADE a habit of joining Harriet and the boys for supper to discuss the business, but she suspected he wouldn't show tonight. Stirring a pot of stew, she stared into the steam and tried to dispel a foul mood by imagining a new future... and revisiting the inn.

She loved her horses, working with them, riding them, but in her old age, that fine, white inn with its columns and gardens would be so peaceful. She tapped the spoon off, laid it on the stove, and hurried to her room to retrieve the postcard.

The beautiful antebellum-style building, gleaming in the sun, would be fit for a queen or a simple businessman vacationing with his family. Her inn would overlook a river or a lake and feature a wide, expansive veranda where ladies in beautiful gowns could have tea in the afternoon or stroll about in the garden on the arm of a handsome gentleman. The more adventurous could wander to the stables and go on long trail rides into the mountains.

That was her future—an easier life. It was hard now, harder than she had expected, but this too would pass. She had to believe that.

Voices from the other side of the curtain ended her musings and she shoved the postcard back into her pocket. Jason and the boys were chatting at the table. She came out, grudgingly happy to see that he had come after all, and returned to her stew.

Well, he *was* really her only friend in Blessings. Of course she wouldn't like that they'd had a heated disagreement.

"I thought you might skip supper with us this evening," she said, stirring and adding a pinch of salt to the meal.

"Well, I, uh…" Jason seemed at a loss for words. Harriet supposed her comment could have been interpreted as either a welcome or a why-did-you-bother. The boys shifted on their feet, perhaps sensing the tension in the air.

She waved her hand. "You're always welcome, Jason."

"Thank you. And I have some news. We've got our first shipment tomorrow. Mosier at the mercantile is shipping some items to the mercantile in Coloma. Dundee has us bringing a shipment back." He grinned widely at Harriet. "So, not everyone has a problem with you trying to wear breeches."

Harriet's lips took on a life of their own, and though she tried to stop it, the slight, grudging smile spread to a full-blown grin.

DURING SUPPER, they discussed sticking to the established routes, but over the next several days, Harriet and Jason would explore some alternative routes. Whit and Wyatt balked at that, they felt they should do some scouting too.

"I suppose it depends on how business flows in," Harriet said, clearing the dishes. "Jason has been getting the word out we're open." Their eyes met. "And apparently, a few people don't mind letting a woman drive a wagon."

His face darkened. "Some places would prefer a woman. And those are the routes I'll drive. Like Volcano. We'd have more business and could be choosier about routes if it wasn't for Reives."

Harriet set the plates in the sink. "Boys, wash these up for me, please. Jason and I are going down to the corral to feed."

"Ah, Ma," Whit protested. "Wyatt and I can do that."

"I know you can." She grabbed her shawl from the hook by

the door. "But Jason and I have some business details to discuss."

CHAPTER SEVENTEEN

JASON KICKED AT A PINE CONE AS HE AND HARRIET MADE THEIR way to the corral, a ten-minute walk. The day was fading and he felt done-in. He'd called on every business in Blessings. Harriet was going to have a lot of freighting to do, but she was also going to miss out on a lot. Her gender bothered more people than he would have thought.

"What do you think most people think, Jason? I mean, about a woman running a freight business."

He shoved his hands in his pockets. He didn't know any other way to be than honest. "Reives is making a dent in things and his horses aren't even here yet."

Harriet's expression changed into something just this side of a thunderstorm. Reives really got under her skin. But then, Jason, too, would truly like to put a boot—

"I won't let him win. We'll make that shipment tomorrow and everything will run smoothly."

"It should. It's not a long trip. The route's established. The wagons are new. Your horses are the best. I'll take one of the boys—"

"I'm driving the route."

Jason bit down on a knee-jerk response and tried to plan his words instead.

"I have to drive it," she continued. "It's the only way to prove I'm capable. I thought you could go by and see Mr. Winslet. Tell him we've come to an agreement with Reives on terms, and he can pick the date for the contest."

All kinds of reasons went through Jason's mind as to why she shouldn't take this first load, but, really— "If we expect to have any business other than a handful of folks in town, maybe you do have to be the one to drive first."

Harriet stopped and spun on him. "Are you being funny?"

"No, I think we have a problem and we have to deal with it. You are capable of driving the route, of picking up and delivering freight. So, do it. Show 'em. You can do it." She puffed up like a rooster and he fought a hard battle to keep the smile off his face. "In the meantime, I'll see Winslet. We'll get this contest done."

Harriet paused, nodded, and then ambled down the path. She pulled something from her pocket and Jason caught up with her. "What's that?" It looked like a postcard.

She absently waved it at him. "A dream. For when I'm old." She gazed at the picture, a large building, a hotel or some such, and then handed it to him. "I've never told anyone about that."

He studied the painted postcard of the Island Hotel. Beautiful place. "You want to go there?"

"I want to open a place like that someday. The horses, the ranch, I love all that, but I want to run a hotel. A fine place where presidents stay, and families come back year after year."

Jason was nonplussed. He'd never suspected. "I—I had no idea—"

"I've never told anyone. Henry didn't even know. Things were so difficult with him I thought I couldn't do anything but build the ranch up for the boys. If that. But Blessings is growing. There's more opportunity here. I just...I just don't want to quit dreaming." Her face took on a disturbing *edge*. "I won't give up. Not ever again."

The steel in her voice was cold and sharp. Jason wondered if Harriet knew the difference anymore between dreaming and grabbing.

CHAPTER EIGHTEEN

SUNLIGHT FLICKERED AND BLINKED THROUGH THE TALL PINES AS Jason rode along in the wagon. A pleasantly warm day, he had truly come to appreciate summer here in the Sierra Mountains. The altitude was high enough that they didn't get unbearable heat in Blessings, but he suspected that meant they'd have their share of snow in the winter. Which would make running the wagons trickier.

He slid his gaze over to Harriet. Hands on the reins, her concentration was intense.

Jason was only a little dismayed to realize he might wind up riding a desk instead of a wagon. Sitting here beside Harriet, he'd come to respect her abilities with her horses. Almost as obedient as trained dogs, they would do anything for her, go anywhere with her. Snow would give her some trouble, but not as much as it might others.

And maybe it was time he used his brains for a change. He'd been a lawman for years, which took courage, and panning for gold relied solely on God's blessings. It might be good for a change to use what God had given him above his shoulders instead of his fists or his gun hand.

"I can tell you're assessing me again, Jason. This is what, our third shipment, you riding shotgun? If I haven't convinced—"

"I was literally just thinking I might be of more use in town, at the desk, dealing with customers, getting new business, driving when I'm needed." She didn't say a word, and after several seconds, puzzled, he continued. "I'd like to go out with Whit and Wyatt one more time. Whit's a little reckless. Anyone gets into trouble, it'll be him, not you. I do think you can handle the rig." Still silence. His frustration flared. "Harriet, have I said something to offend you? Am I going to talk to myself all the way to Coloma and back?"

"Easy girls." The road dropped here at a fairly steep descent. She pulled back on the reins, controlling the four horses easily, making sure things were in hand, then she leaned toward Jason. "I just was appreciating the compliments, was all."

"One usually does that with a *thank you*, not silence."

She ignored the sarcasm. "You sure you want to sit in the office?"

He scratched his nose and gazed out at the view of the valley peeking between the trees. "Yeah, some. I'd like the chance to use my brains and not my brawn so much. I'm getting older. Driving a wagon is a young man's—young *woman's*—game."

"What are you, thirty?" she mocked.

"Three. Thirty-three. And I'm not getting any younger. I've got a little money and a business I believe in. It's time I start making some long-term plans."

"Like marriage and a family?"

"It would be nice." An awkward silence fell between them then. Or maybe only he thought it was awkward. Maybe she didn't give a gnat's wing about his plans.

"Got anybody in mind?"

The question surprised him. He hadn't expected her to ask. He took a long look at her. Her raised chin, pert, sort of upturned nose, ramrod straight posture, and all that blonde hair shimmering in the sun. She was a picture. "No," he said flatly, maybe a little hopelessly. It wasn't a lie. Jason didn't quite know what to think of Harriet, and she obviously didn't think about him at all. Would she, in time?

Only time will tell, eh, Harriet? Only time will tell.

———

ARMS CROSSED, Harriet leaned on the post in front of the mercantile and surveyed Archie Reives's horses as they trotted down the street. A remuda of ten bustled by, ranging from sorrels to pintos. The ship voyage had been none too kind to the animals, and the trip from San Francisco to here hadn't helped. Painfully underweight, she could count their ribs as they trotted past.

Of course, a couple of weeks on good feed and hay and they would be ready to run...ready to pull some freight. She wasn't going to write off Archie Reives just yet, but she was willing to bet her teams had this contest in hand.

"Not much to look at, but he's already getting business."

She spun on Jason. "What? Using those half-starved nags?"

He shrugged, apparently lacking an explanation.

"That's insane," she fumed, whirling back around and craning to see the herd disappear down the street. "Why?"

"Simply because he's a man." Dundee stepped out of the mercantile carrying a package wrapped in brown paper. "A foolish reason, but mates tend to stick together. You'll have to show them what you're capable of, Harriet. Give them a better reason to trust you."

———

HARRIET TOOK THE SUGGESTION LITERALLY. The next afternoon, she, Whit, and Wyatt led their horses down Main Street, using only bridles and halters, no other tack. Riding a horse bareback and leading one, they each had groomed the animals to stunning perfection, and they glistened like new pennies. In front of the mercantile, the surprising troop stopped, Harriet whistled a command, and the animals backed up several feet.

By now, a curious crowd was forming. Men grinned and elbowed each other. Women peered between shoulders and armpits. Children peeked between legs and climbed into wagons for better views.

This time, Whit whistled a long, high-pitched call, and all the horses pivoted on their back legs to the right. The crowd *oohed* and *aahed,* and Harriet smiled. Wyatt whistled three short bursts and the horses pivoted back. In rapid succession, Harriet whistled, then Whit, and then Wyatt. Like well-trained soldiers, the horses responded immediately, backing up, turning...and then bowing their heads to the crowd.

A wild cheer went up from the onlookers and Harriet's spirits soared. She raised her arms into the air like a showman in the circus ring and then pointed at her sons. The applause and shouts from the audience intensified. Clapping, she spotted Reives watching from the crowd and knew she couldn't afford to let slip by the chance to rub a little salt in his wounds.

"Folks," she yelled, "Everybody." The crowd quieted a little. "The Pullen Freight Company is open for business. Please think of us for all your shipping needs. We've got the finest and, obviously, smartest horses in Blessings! Shoot, in California!"

Reives sneered and Harriet merely dipped her chin in appreciation of his attention.

"Showmanship certainly helps, Harriet." Jason laid down a pencil and leaned back in his chair. The light from outside silhouetted her nicely in the doorway—floppy hat she'd taken to wearing, hourglass figure, and fraying golden braid—he coughed and quickly sat back up. "You made good time. All the way to Nugget and back in four hours."

"It's not a hard trail."

"We picked up three new accounts today."

Harriet commenced peeling off her riding gloves and turned back around to watch the boys taking her team out of the harness. "That's good news." She motioned at her teenagers. "How are they doing?"

"Fine. I'm not riding with them on the short hauls anymore. They can handle them."

"I knew they'd be all right."

"I think you're pushing them too hard, though."

"There's no school right now," she said over her shoulder. "Won't hurt them to work."

"But they're boys. They're here sunup to sundown like us. Don't you think they should have a little fun?"

She spun back around, and for an instant, he thought she might lob a glove at him. "Fun? We don't have time for fun. There's too much work to do. We've got to build up this business and beat Reives. I'll have some *fun* when we win Mr. Winslet's contract."

Jason knew there was no arguing with her. Danged if she wasn't driven. "Speaking of Reives, I ran into him today. He said your circus act on Main Street didn't impress him."

"I don't care what he thinks." She snatched off her hat. "In fact, I hope he keeps taking me for granted. We'll walk away with this contest."

"I hope you're right, Harriet. I hope you're right."

She set her gloves and hat on a shelf just inside the door and sat down opposite him. "Let's divvy up the routes for tomorrow. I need to get home and get supper started."

Jason studied her for a second more, drawn to her, bewitched by her, but deeply frustrated with her. *Lord, is she ever going to see past all that hurt to...what's right in front of her?* He dragged a clipboard over in front of him. "All righty. Here's what we've got..."

CHAPTER NINETEEN

HARRIET PULLED THE HORSES TO A STOP AND STUDIED THE rushing river. A few days ago, it had only been a moderately stout creek. Today, it exceeded its banks, and debris was sweeping down the middle of it.

But she couldn't turn back. This was supposed to be one of the easier routes to Fiddle Town. Admitting defeat today to the angry water would cost her too much. And not in dollars. She tapped her foot on the floorboard, as if debating, but this was not an argument. Only a nervous pause. Yes, it would be smarter to double back and cross upstream where the water was lower, but that was longer. Hours and miles out of the way.

The swirling, tumultuous river mocked her. Resolute, she swallowed her fear and slapped the leather across the horses. The wagon bumped and jostled forward into the water. It rose quickly. She could feel the wagon fishtailing as it lost contact here and there with the rocky bottom.

Nearly halfway through, in the deepest part, the back wheel rolled over a rock and the jarring thud nearly knocked her teeth loose. The pain and her growing sense of disquiet lit her temper. "Come on, come on," she growled to the team of horses, "let's get this over with."

She loosened the reins a little and the animals responded by pulling harder against the current. The wagon suddenly shifted hard to the right then started outright floating—all four of the wheels lost their ground. *It could tip,* Harriet thought, alarmed.

She slapped the reins again and the lead to Jessie Bell came loose. For a moment, she was thunderstruck watching the free end slide into the water as if it had simply been unhitched. There was no way to control both horses now. Her heart pounded like a crazed drummer. She dropped the useless rein and took Dollar's rein in both hands. "Come on, boy! Get us out of here."

Oh, God, Jessie Bell's got to follow him or we'll all drown—

The wagon shifted perpendicular to the horses, tugging ferociously on them, straining the leather. Jessie Bell neighed in panic, spreading her fear to Dollar. The gelding's eyes rolled wildly and the mare clawed for purchase on the bottom, but the water kept pushing. Harriet felt the wagon heave. It lifted and snapped the pole with a thunderous crack, freeing the horses.

Harriet leaped into the rapids as the right side of the wagon surged up, flipped, and almost instantly submerged. For a flick of a second, the world was silent as the ice-cold water surrounded her and stole her breath. The horses pawed frantically at the rocks so close to their feet, and they tugged on their harness, working against each other in their panic.

Harriet splashed and kicked and broke to the surface. Gasping, coughing, she swam madly toward the shore. The current shocked her with its strength, proving itself by slamming her into a boulder. Stars danced in her head, blackness threatened—

"Don't fight the current," someone yelled. "Swim toward the shore and I'll get ya downstream!"

Oh, God, please don't let me die—Harriet sputtered and choked as a wave hit her in the face. She swam hard, desperate for the shore. *Please don't let me die here,* she prayed. The water roared and rushed around her. The chill sank into her bones. The waves rolled over her with astonishing power and she felt like a leaf in a hurricane.

"All right, reach for me! Reach for me!"

Harriet blinked, tried to follow the sound of the voice, and shoved out her arm. There! A man on the shore had anchored himself on a fallen tree that extended into the water and was reaching for Harriet. She extended her arm as far as it would go and then stretched even more—

"Gotcha!" Fingers, warm and firm, grasped her wrist. "All right, paddle, girl, paddle. Come toward me and—hey, throw me the other end of that strap."

Harriet still had the broken reins in her hand. She kicked, but it seemed her legs couldn't respond as fast as she wanted. She could hardly feel them. So cold. Stiffly, she whipped the reins, popping the other end out of the water. The hand on her wrist tightened, tension on the strap increased, and the water slowly loosened its grip. Ground collided with her feet and she pushed toward the shore, gasping and coughing.

"There ya go."

Dry land. Harriet choked and sputtered and scrambled clumsily over rocks to the shore, collapsing to her hands and knees. One end of the leather strap was tangled around her wrist.

"Take a minute, get your bearings." A hand whacked her on the back. "Cough out the river."

She did, three more times, and finally felt better. She took several clear breaths, grateful the weight of the water was off her chest. *My horses!* The thought launched through her like a

Chinese rocket and she looked up at the man who had helped. "My horses?"

"Made it to shore. They're fine."

With relief, Harriet fell over on her hip and studied her rescuer. A short, heavy man with oddly delicate hands, he tipped his worn hat at her then started slipping into a pair of leather work gloves. "Oh, gee," he said, snatching a bandana from his pants pocket and touching it to her forehead. "You're bleeding."

Harriet held the cloth in place, too exhausted to worry how much she was bleeding. Slowly, though, the thundering headache convinced her she'd lost a round with a rock.

"I'm Charly Parkhurst, by the way."

"And I'm lucky you happened along." Harriet grimaced at the raging river. Her wagon and its contents were likely all the way to San Francisco by now. "Wish you could have saved my wagon and the freight." Dang, that was a setback. Teeth-chattering, dripping wet, she stood and offered her hand to Charly. "Thank you."

He accepted with a smile. "My pleasure. *I* wouldn't have crossed there, but you almost made it." Buck-toothed with heavy brows, he was far from handsome, but he was also about the most beautiful thing Harriet had seen in a long time. He frowned at something and reached for her wrist. Squinting, he pulled the rein free and raised it to eye level. That heavy brow creased with open suspicion. "That's queer. No reason it should break like that."

Forgetting her injured head, Harriet snatched the leather from her rescuer and examined it. *A nice, clean edge.* "It was cut." Rage coursed through her.

Reives?

"That would be my guess," Charly said slowly. "That could have killed you. You might be lucky it gave up in the water.

Otherwise, you could have gone over and been crushed by the wagon."

Harriet shivered. *Would he go to such lengths?*

Movement in the trees caught her eye and she and Charly both whipped their heads up. A man on a horse spurred the animal and took off over the ridge. Obscured by the branches, Harriet could only see he was not a small man. Larger, thicker, he put her in mind of Magruder, but she couldn't be sure.

"Hey, my rig's up there." Charly took off at a run. "I'll be back."

CHAPTER TWENTY

To Harriet's relief, Charly returned several minutes later with a blanket and the confirmation that his rig and horses were intact. "If that fella was the cause of this trouble, he wasn't here to bother with me." He helped Harriet round up Dollar and Jessie Bell and tied them to the back of his wagon. "So, where were you headed?" he asked, climbing to the driver's seat.

Harriet joined him and re-wrapped the blanket. "Blessings."

"Ah, well, that's not too far outta my way." He released his hand brake, slapped the reins, and let the horses take off at an easy trot. "I'll take you on in."

"Thanks. I appreciate it." She shivered beneath the blanket and knew it would take a while to get her warmth back. The freight was gone. The wagon was gone. Her head hurt like Dollar had kicked her. And she had to face Jason with the news.

"Who did you make mad enough to cut your reins?"

"One man in Blessings thinks I took his job. Another man

knows he's going to lose a race to me. If I win, I get the freight contract from the mine in town."

Charly shook his head. "Don't neither one seem like reason enough to kill a body, but men are crazy."

Amen to that.

"I saw you come down the hill. You almost turned around. Why didn't you?"

"You wouldn't understand."

"Try me."

"Too many men in town think I can't drive a wagon because I'm a woman. I didn't want to turn back because..."

"Because of your pride." Charly produced a stogie from his breast pocket, lit it with impressive skill while driving the horses, then tossed the match aside. He puffed happily on the cigar for a moment before speaking again. "Ambition isn't a bad thing 'lessen it makes you foolish. In this case, it might have saved your life, but don't bank on it all the time. Do what's wise and you'll live longer."

Harriet had to chuckle. Certainly, sage advice. For no good reason, it led her to a question. "What were you doing beside the river?"

"Funny, that. I had just stopped to take a whizz." He cut his eyes at Harriet. "You didn't see me?"

"No."

"Good. I mean, that would have been..." he left off and Harriet nodded, glad they didn't have that between them. "And about being a woman," Charly continued, "you can drive a wagon as good as a man, probably better than most. Just be the best *you* can be though, and don't worry about what everybody else thinks. You can't live your life trying to meet their expectations. Make and exceed your own."

"You're right, I know. I'm just anxious to get back on my feet again. My first husband lost everything we had. I'm starting over."

"Thems the breaks, sometimes."

Harriet nodded but didn't say anything. Charly was doing enough conversing for the the both of them.

"You've got good-lookin' horses," he said. "Think you'll beat that other fella?"

"Yes." She didn't bother to hide her determined tone.

"Hell-bent on it, huh?"

"Oh, yes."

"Be careful. They don't call it blind ambition for nothin'. Might change your life. Might kill ya."

Harriet *was* ambitious, but there was nothing blind about it. She could see clearer now than she ever had. In fact, the path before her was lit with torches, as far as she was concerned. And if Archie Reives stood on that path, she was going to roll right over him.

CHAPTER TWENTY-ONE

THE RUMBLING RATTLE OF A WAGON SNATCHED JASON'S GAZE from his paperwork to the regulator clock on the wall. Only four thirty. Neither Harriet nor the boys were due back yet.

"Thank you, Charly." Harriet's voice. Jason slapped his pencil down and hurried outside. He found her standing between Dollar and Jessie Bell, waving to a departing wagon. Not their wagon. And even from the rear, Jason could tell something was wrong. Harriet's hair was a mess—looked to still be damp, in fact—and an old Indian blanket was draped over her shoulders. The horses, too, looked a little worse for wear, and some of their tack was missing.

"Harriet, something happen?"

Her shoulders sagged, but almost instantly, she pulled them back up, raised her chin, and walked the horses around so she could face him. The swelling cut on her forehead, red and raw and turning an angry blue on the edges, made his heart lurch. He stepped up to her, clutching her and lifting her face to him, his abruptness sending the horses into a nervous prance. "Holy cow, what happened? Are you all right...and your clothes are wet?" He pressed his hand to the base of her neck, gathering up some of her damp hair.

Swatting him off, she stepped away from him to bring the horses back in hand. "I'm fine. I'm fine." But she dropped her eyes and Jason thought he could guess the rest.

"You lost the whole shipment and the wagon, didn't you?" He kicked himself for making the careless statement and reined in his temper. She was more important than any freight. "Not that it matters. Tell me if you're all right or not."

She looked indignant, but it was a front, he knew. "I'm fine. Just hit my head on a rock...in the middle of a flooded creek." She deflated a little. "While the wagon was sinking and our freight was washing down river to San Francisco Bay."

She could have drowned. He pivoted away from her, turning his back so he could collect himself. Maybe she didn't have any business driving a wagon after all. Tension snaked up his shoulders and clear through his scalp. He rubbed the muscles in his neck with one hand while the other tapped his thigh. Every time she climbed in a wagon now he was going to worry about her. *Lord, this woman is going to put me in an early grave.*

He took a deep breath and faced her, peering at her with as withering a gaze as he could manage. The longer he stared at her, though, the higher Harriet's chin rose.

If she isn't the most stubborn, the most prideful— "Tell me one thing: was it avoidable?"

Harriet's face went slack. She'd probably expected a lot of questions, but this was the crux of the matter. She flailed for words for a moment, then finally managed, "If I'd been willing to turn around and lose three hours, then yes."

Jason's temper roared free. "Three hours? That's what you would have saved? Look what you risked." She flinched at his tone but didn't cower, and he didn't care. "You could have drowned. You were alone, Harriet. You can't take chances like that if you're alone. The boys could be without their mother right now. I could be—" *Lost. Alone. Grieving.* "Without my partner." He didn't want to leave it like that. "I could have lost a friend today," he said softly.

The stubborn lift to her chin stayed, but only for a moment. She shook her head and handed him the one remaining led to Jessie Bell. "Help me put them up."

He stared at the single rein. "Where's the rest of it?" He checked the horse over, tugging on the harness, buckles, and straps.

Harriet closed her eyes. "It was cut."

"What?"

She peered at him with one eye. "Promise me you won't get mad."

"I'll promise no such thing. Besides, you get mad all the time. Why can't I?"

"Because, in truth, I'm not likely to shoot anybody. If you're angry, this could escalate, and I..." She trailed off, looking puzzled. "And I wouldn't want anyone to get hurt." She said the words carefully, as if choosing them one at a time with great deliberation.

Jason had no time for this. "Harriet, you need to speak plain. What happened?"

"Somebody cut the rein. If it had broken on the road, I would have lost control of the team, maybe even fallen under the wagon. Taking the river crossing at high water was a bad idea, but it may have saved my life."

Jason stared at her, disbelieving. Surely Reives wasn't this stupid.

"See, there"—she snatched Jessie Bell's line from him—"that look." She marched off, shaking her head and dragging the startled horses. "That look tells me you won't back down from any trouble."

Back down? He was going to *find* it. Harriet could have

been hurt. And what if something like this happened to the boys?

"Did you see anything? Before or after?" His voice was cold. She didn't answer right away and he followed her into the barn. "Answer me, Harriet. If someone tried to hurt you, how do we know they won't go after the boys?" She whipped her head around with a gasp. Jason nodded. "I'll go after them right now, but tell me anything I might need to know."

She licked her lips. "Afterward, Charly and I saw a man through the trees. I didn't get a good look, Jason. You have to understand that...but he reminded me of Magruder."

He laid a reassuring hand on her shoulder. "I'll go find the boys and make sure they're all right. Then I'll go see Magruder."

———

HARRIET HAD WANTED to go with Jason, but something in his face told her she'd pushed him about as far as she should dare. He'd promised he'd bring Whit and Wyatt home safe and she'd let him ride out with that being the last word.

Weary, overwhelmed, and embarrassingly weepy, she brushed down Dollar and Jessie Bell and then closed up the office. Had someone tried to hurt her? The idea was surreal. She was not, however, a simpering little fool who wouldn't take the possibility of sabotage seriously. They would watch each other's backs. They would go armed. And Jason would...

Jason would what? Take care of them?

Her thoughts were a tangled mess that didn't straighten out as she walked home, nor when she cut some venison hanging over the fireplace for dinner. She went through the familiar actions of preparing the meal, but her mind was roiling with questions and fears.

You were alone, Harriet. You can't take chances like that if you're alone. The boys could be without their mother right now. I could be—

Harriet had the surest sense he had wanted to say something different than *partner* or *friend*. But what? And she had realized with shock that she didn't want Jason looking for trouble because *he* might get hurt.

Of course, she didn't want him to get hurt. He was too valuable as a partner. And the fact remained if she and the boys were in danger, Jason was a good man to have around.

He was certainly useful.

Pouring a little water over the venison—she didn't even remember putting it in the pot—she thought back to Henry and all the pain his selfish actions had caused. She relived the agony of saying goodbye to her children. Recalled the letters from Katie that said she was all right yet left so much unspoken. A girl needs her mother, especially at this age.

And all of this heartbreak was a man's fault. No—

She straightened up, angry with herself for passing the blame. In truth, all this was Harriet's fault. She'd let herself become dependent on a man she *knew* was weak and apt to fall. Married to her and a bottle and cheating on them both with cards.

She stared up at the ceiling. *Never again, God, will I be that simple, that trusting, that vulnerable. Just help me get back on my feet, Lord, please, and let me do it on my own. Jason—Jason has to stay at arm's length. But we do need him.*

As if in response to her plea, she heard his voice mixed with the laughter of her boys. He had brought them home safe! Practically skipping, she raced to meet them on the porch.

———

HARRIET LEARNED over dinner conversation that Jason had downplayed her day's troubles. He'd met the boys about an hour out of town and rode back with them, getting the details of their run and sharing, matter-of-factly, Harriet's. A famished crew they all were, and exhausted. They scarfed up the venison cutlets in gravy, but then Whit and Wyatt headed off to bed early. A sure sign they were tired, and Harriet grudgingly considered Jason's admonition to let them find time to rest and have some fun.

She laid her napkin on the table and looked up at him. His piercing gaze startled her at first, but then she allowed—or couldn't stop—a quick moment to bask in those stunning blue eyes, note the razor stubble on his chin and the way a stray golden hair curled over his left ear.

She blinked and stood to clear the dishes, but he touched her hand, stopping her and sending her pulse off to the races. "Let's you and me take a walk, Harriet." He rose to retrieve his hat from the hook by the door. "Come on. The dishes can wait."

"All right." She commanded her heart to slow its break-neck pace, but it willfully disobeyed her.

They ambled down the path that led to the river and Harriet smiled at the lightning bugs coming to life around them. She knew, though, this wasn't going to be a happy conversation. Jason's shoulders were stiff, his face tight. She was too tired for another lecture and too tired to argue over it. She did, however, deserve it. Her foolishness had not only cost them the wagon but the freight too. No doubt, tomorrow, tongues would be wagging.

"I told the boys what happened but didn't make any big shakes of it."

"Good. Thank you."

"The truth is, though"—he touched her shoulder and turned her toward him—"it is a big deal. I have to go see

Mosier tomorrow and tell him we lost his shipment. We're down a wagon now, as well. And if you think Reives isn't going to make some hay with this fiasco—"

"All right, all right." Angry, she spun away from him and crossed her arms. "I messed up. Royally."

"You're dang straight you did. Harriet, if you don't get that grudge of yours—that chip off your shoulder—you're going to keep making mistakes like this."

Every word he said made her feel like a spike getting hammered and hammered and hammered into the ground.

"Harriet, your bitterness is making you reckless. Henry was no prize catch. He did you wrong. Caused you some pretty severe hardship. Well, look past it, or it's going to ruin you."

She gasped and spun on him. "Look past it? Get over it? What do you think I'm trying to do?"

"I think you're scared to death of being left again. And the way to prevent it is to keep everybody away who can hurt you."

"I'm scared to death of not being able to provide for my children." Her voice rose, shrill and sharp. "I'm scared to death I might have to pawn them off somewhere while I go and try to build our lives again. You have no idea how that ripped out my heart. *Those* are the things I'm afraid of."

"Harriet, shhhh." Jason gently laid his hands on her shoulders. "I'm sorry. I'm sorry. I didn't mean to make it sound like it was nothing. It's just that you don't have to do all this on your own."

Harriet fixated on the warmth of his hands grasping her shoulders, his mass towering over her protectively, the urgency of some undecipherable message burning in his eyes.

"You don't have to keep pushing me away. Harriet, do you know why I left Sundown?"

She gulped and shook her head. Suddenly, she didn't think she wanted to know.

"It killed me watching you struggle every day, trying to hold your family and your ranch together while Henry was out carousing and drinking. It killed me because I love you, but I couldn't tell you that while he was alive."

CHAPTER TWENTY-TWO

SHOCK SLICED FROM THE TOP OF HARRIET'S HEAD DOWN TO HER toes. *Love? He loves me?* A moment of burning silence ignited the air between them, but in the end, Harriet slowly pulled away. "I'm sorry. If I ever did anything to encourage you—"

"No, you didn't. Not a thing." His face hardened and he straightened up.

"No matter what you think, Jason, about my reasons or my motivations, you have to understand I will never depend on a man again. Ever. All I want is my family back with me. The boys and Katie. That's all. Maybe, when I make that happen, and I'm reasonably comfortable, I'll think differently."

"You mean you'll want a man who's a lapdog?"

"What? No. I—I don't know what..." She trailed off.

"A husband should be a partner, not a man who lords things over you."

"A partner?" She considered the idea but doubted a man was capable of ever truly partnering with a woman. She did not want to hurt Jason though, any more than she already had. He loved her and she was deeply moved by his affections

—more than she ought to be—but she was also not about to waver from her goals. "Well, we're partners now. Why don't we just see—give things time."

He swiped a big hand over his mouth, scratched his nose, and pushed his hat back an inch. The actions of a man buying time to think. He looked up at the purple sky and sighed. "You may hate me for this, Harriet, but I have to know."

He swept her small frame into her arms, held her to him, and pressed his lips to hers. Lightning arced between them, jolting her to life. His crushing arms around her, his broad chest beneath her fingers, the heat of his lips on hers intoxicated her. She felt drunk, breathless...

He deepened the kiss, and she surrendered. A vortex of emotions swirled in her mind, whipping up torrents of desire. Her hands slid up his chest, around to the back of his neck, combed through his soft, curly hair. She couldn't think. She seemed capable only of succumbing to her senses.

Her heart hammered in her chest and she moaned with fear and pleasure at his touch, his heat, his control. She was lightheaded, overwhelmed, incapable of thought, savoring the taste of him, moving toward him as the tips of his teeth gently teased her lips. She needed him like she needed air. Desire burned in her, hot as the earth's core. He took another kiss, feeding the passion. Her knees gave way and he caught her, his arms tightening like bands of steel.

And like a drunk starved of whiskey, Harriet wanted Jason and only he could slake this thirst he'd created in her. Only him...

Slowly, reluctantly, he pulled away. Rational thought crashed back into Harriet's head and she realized...realized her vulnerability. She slipped from his grasp, ashamed of her reaction.

Only him? No, no...

The spell broken, she could hardly remember thinking it, but her body still sang like a telegraph wire, her breathing wouldn't slow. She laid her hands on her cheeks, hot as stoves. "I can't believe I...reacted like that." She wouldn't look at him. What must he think? She tried to explain—to them both. "You have no idea how long it's been since a man held me like that." Her throat tightened with tears and longing. "You shouldn't read too much into it."

Jason cupped her chin but she resisted looking at him and he didn't force her. "Harriet, I'm no expert, but I've kissed a few women." He took a deep breath and whispered in her ear, "Not a one has ever felt like that in my arms."

"Jason, don't, please—" Tears threatened. What was the matter with her?

"It's all right, Harriet. I've got my answer. You felt it. I know you did. And that'll do for now."

———

HARRIET TOSSED and turned that night in bed, roiling with disappointment and desire. Jason had stoked a blaze in her. She burned to be in his arms and hated herself for the yearning he stirred. When he'd whispered, *"Not a one has ever felt like that in my arms,"* his breath in her ear had caressed her skin like a lover's touch.

Of course, nearly dying in that flooded creek today jarred loose my self-control, is all, she rationalized. *A close call with death would prompt anyone to reach out and grab hold of life. I'm merely overwrought.*

She'd hugged the boys tighter before they'd gone to bed... and she'd kissed Jason like the emotionally starved widow she was. Starving but desperately glad to be alive. And, oh, how he made her feel alive.

The touch of his lips, his arms, his breath...

She growled and rolled over in her bed, beating her pillow into submission. *He makes me feel alive, Lord, and yearn for something I don't think I've ever had. But not now. Not now. I need to put Katie and the boys first. Then—then I'll think about Jason.*

CHAPTER TWENTY-THREE

FULLY AWARE SLEEP WOULD NOT BE POSSIBLE AFTER WHAT HAD just happened with Harriet, Jason stormed toward the saloon. If he was much of a drinker, this would be the night to toss back a few.

He'd walked Harriet back to the cabin and neither one of them had said a word, not even good night. She had looked pained, at war with herself, Jason reasoned, if he could measure anything by her response to his kiss. Maybe it was dangerous being cocky, but he knew one thing for sure: she wasn't immune to him.

Give me patience and help me wear her down.

The saloon's jangling piano echoed jarringly down the quiet street. It almost convinced him to turn around and go home. He wasn't really in the mood for alcohol or company, but the thought of lying in bed thinking about Harriet held no appeal either. Just then, he heard a kind of harsh, barking laugh. It rose above the other saloon noise and he stopped in his tracks.

Reives.

With the emotional turmoil over Harriet, he'd dang near

forgotten about what happened at the river. Had Reives been involved? Had Magruder cut the lead rein? Harriet had a sharp eye, and Jason was inclined to trust it. If she thought she saw the big man, she probably did. Magruder, though, didn't strike Jason as the kind who thought of such underhanded tricks on his own. A trail of reasoning led back to Reives.

Jason marched up to the batwings and peered in. Reives was in his usual seat, last table on the side, back to the wall, dealing cards. And as luck would have it, Magruder was at the bar tossing back a shot. Jason drummed his fingers on the doors for a moment, then pushed through them.

He moved slowly among the smoke and laughter, trying not to draw Reives's attention. He wanted words with Magruder first. With natural ease, he settled beside the big man and nodded at Ellie. "Just a beer." Magruder, now holding a full mug of ale, paused it halfway to his mouth. Jason smiled. "You look a little rattled, Magruder. Nervous even. Why would you be nervous?"

The man guzzled his drink, set down the mug, and wiped the foam from his ragged beard. "I don't know what you're talking about."

"Then let me speak plain." Jason slipped closer to Magruder and lowered his voice. "It's pretty obvious Harriet's lead rein was cut."

"I don't know what you're talking about."

"That would be really good, Magruder. Because if I thought you had cut it, that you purposely tried to harm a young widow woman, I just don't believe I could contain myself." Jason inched closer and lowered his voice even more. "If I thought you might be stupid enough to try it again, I'd bury you, and no one would ever find your bones. Then I'd go after the man who put you up to it." Jason stared at Magruder, waiting him out.

Several seconds passed. Finally, Magruder swallowed and

licked his lips nervously. "I'm leaving town. You're having this talk with the wrong man."

"That's good." Jason slapped Magruder on the back as if they were enjoying a delightful, friendly conversation. "That's real good. Leaving in the morning, I suspect."

"Y—yes."

"And one last thing. Were you taking orders?"

Magruder took forever to answer, but Jason knew he would. "Yeah."

"And I know who it is, don't I?"

"Yeah."

Jason's beer arrived. Done with Magruder, he slipped two bits over to the bartender and pivoted toward Reives. He had no doubt from where Magruder had gotten his orders. Jason strolled over and took the empty chair on Reives's right.

Dealing cards, he barely paused at the new player. "You're playing?"

Jason set his beer on the table and nudged his hat back. "Yeah."

"Fifty dollar buy-in."

Jason fished some coins from his breast pocket and laid them on the table as Reives dealt him in, then he settled back and watched the bug intently. "Magruder's leaving in the morning."

Reives's right hand launching the cards hitched slightly but his expression didn't change. "What's that to me?"

"I guess you heard Harriet had a little accident this afternoon."

"I had not heard."

"Then let me fill you in." Jason gathered up his cards and fanned them out just enough to see the suits. "Someone cut her lead rein. If she hadn't been crossing Fiddle Town Creek when it happened, she might have been jerked off the wagon and run over."

"That would have been a terrible tragedy." Reives anted up, and the other players followed suit.

"Yes, a double tragedy."

"Double. Why?"

"Because I would hunt down the man responsible and bring him to justice." Uneasy glances ricocheted around the table as the other players sensed the tension. Jason kept his manner easy and calm. He plucked two cards from his hand and laid them on the table. "I'll take two." Reives obliged, and Jason lazily sorted his hand.

"You know, maybe the lady just has no business driving a wagon. If she can't cross a creek..."

"Little hard to, with your tack dangling in the water."

"Things will happen along the route. She should be prepared for them."

Jason's fingers itched to clench Reives's skinny throat. "I used to be in law enforcement, Reives. As a matter of fact, we've met before."

"Really. I don't recall."

"And it can stay that way as long as Harriet stays safe." Reives's gaze flicked up and Jason smiled. "Anything else happens to her, you're going to recall right much about a hot June in Atchison, oh, about four or five years ago."

The muscles in Reives's face tightened and Jason knew he had hit the nerve. There were a lot of warrants outstanding on a certain confidence man and swindler.

Bets went around the table. Someone raised. They matched. Players folded. Oddly, the hand came down to Jason and Reives.

"I don't think you're the kind of man who bluffs, Jason, but I've got a winning hand."

"Then I call."

Reives laid down a straight flush. Jason sucked on his teeth and shrugged. "Not bad." He fanned out his own cards. "But it doesn't beat royalty." Reives dragged back from the table with a heavy sigh.

Jason waited a moment, then removed his hat and raked the pot into it. Without any further ado, he rose and studied his enemy for a moment. "We understand each other, Reives?"

"I believe you have made yourself crystal clear, Jason."

CHAPTER TWENTY-FOUR

GRUMBLING BENEATH HER BREATH, HARRIET BENT DOWN AND lit the office stove, eager to knock off the chill. Usually Jason did this, but she had beat him in this morning. Troubled, she wanted to go over the books and update herself on their financial situation. Word had spread, no doubt with Reives's help, that Harriet had lost a load. Pullen Freight Company customers had not dried up, but three had backed out, sending their business to Reives.

She slid the coffee pot over to the center of the stove, sat down at the desk, and pulled the ledger from the drawer. Intently flipping pages to the most recent date, she jumped at a knock on the office door. At this hour? "Come in."

To her astonishment, Reives, in all his gangly and cheap-suit glory, sashayed in. Harriet wasn't thrilled to see him. "You're up early."

"Haven't been to bed yet." He wandered over and touched the pot. Twice.

"I just put it on."

"Oh. Aren't you going to ask me what I'm doing here?" He

leaned back on the wall and crossed long, skinny arms across his chest.

"What are you doing here?"

"I came to make you an offer. I want to buy your business."

"Buy my business? What makes you think I want to sell? Especially to you?"

"You're losing business. Everyone knows you can handle horses, but wagons are a different story. You're in over your head. Sell to me. I'll pay a fair price and you can start something different. A bakery or some such. And I won't have any competition."

That's when it dawned on her. "You know you're going to lose."

He scoffed, coming off the wall. "I know I'm going to win. And when I do, I still have to compete with you. I'd rather not."

Harriet drummed her fingers on the ledger, wondering what Reives was after. "So you just want to shut down the competition." She smiled. "If you win."

He nodded.

"Well, I'm not selling."

"Then how about an alternative offer? All or nothing."

"Meaning?"

"Whoever wins this contest gets all the competitor's assets."

That was intriguing, but Harriet tried not to look too interested. "So, when I win, you're out of business. I get your wagons and your horses." She'd seen his horses lately. They were coming along. Not as nice as her remuda, but they could be useful.

"And the cash assets as well."

She couldn't stop her eyes from widening in shock.

Reives slid his hands into his pockets and shrugged. "I said all or nothing. Now, of course, that door swings both ways."

"How much cash are we talking about?"

"I have eighteen thousand dollars in the bank—well..." He shrugged. "Not exactly in the bank. Let's say *on hand*."

Harriet and Jason together had nearly eight. Of course, only about a thousand of that was hers, but she'd provided her horses and manpower.

"Now, I know you and Jason don't have that much. But, like I said, this will get you out of my hair."

On the surface, this seemed like a reasonable enough wager. Harriet's freight team was going to win. Yet she hesitated and realized it was because she knew this might not please Jason.

"I understand, of course, if you need to run this by Jason and get his approval."

Harriet resented the obvious poke at her pride. "Mr. Reives, I have to make a run to Volcano this morning." She rose and sauntered over to him, holding his gaze. His eyes smoldered for a moment when she stopped directly in front of them, but then she reached behind him for her hat and driver's gloves. He cleared his throat, perhaps dispelling a little embarrassment, and she smiled, pleased with herself. "I don't have time to discuss this right now." She slipped into a glove and offered her hand. "But I tentatively accept your offer."

———

JASON GRABBED the smoking coffee pot and snatched his hand back, shaking off the pain. *Well, of course it's hot, it's smoking.* He grabbed the dishcloth hanging with the mugs on the wall, doubled it up, and took the burning coffee pot outside. He set it on the rain barrel next to the door and surveyed the yard. The Conestoga was missing, and Bo and Booker were missing from the corral.

Surely, she didn't...

"Whit," Jason bellowed, storming into the barn.

The young man was oiling some harness tack and looked up, eyes wide as silver dollars. "Yes, sir?"

"Where's your ma? Tell me she didn't take the shipment to—"

"Volcano. She said you'd be mad but that you shouldn't worry."

Livid, Jason grabbed a saddle off the wall, the tack to go with it, and headed for the corral. Before he left, he strapped on his Colt.

———

HARRIET HAD a good enough head start on him that she would probably already be in Volcano by the time he caught up with her. Maybe it wouldn't be too late. Maybe he could keep her out of trouble. He grumbled about her stubborn streak and prayed for her safety all the way, cutting a four-hour route by wagon down to two-and-a-half with a single horse. Riley was going to be one tired palomino, but Volcano was no place for a woman alone.

The trouble that place bred preying on his mind, Jason took every shortcut he could think of or had heard about. He hit the little hovel of a town at about noon. Squatting along the banks of Credo Creek, it had one Main Street, and he rode straight down the middle, grimacing at the condition of the settlement. It only boasted about a hundred residents, but many of them had served in the same unit during the war with Mexico. This bunch had seen the atrocity at the Alamo and then ridden across the border to exact vengeance. Few had faulted them for their behavior then, but these men hadn't left the war behind. Gun and knife fights were as common in this mountain town as raindrops in April.

Jason passed a few folks working their claims, knee-deep in icy water, swirling hope in their pans. They studied him with wary, narrowed eyes. He dipped his head nonchalantly and kept Riley to a trot. A moment later, he pulled up in front of a shack that passed for a mercantile but did not dismount. This end of town was eerily quiet. He nudged the horse around back and spotted the wagon. The boxes were sitting on the landing.

But no Harriet.

A shrill scream exploded from the trees behind the store. Jason snatched his Colt Walker free and spurred Riley.

CHAPTER TWENTY-FIVE

HE AND THE BIG-CHESTED PALOMINO BURST IN ON A CIRCLE OF four men. One had Harriet stretched across his shoulders and was spinning about with her while the three other men leaped and clawed and grabbed for her. Riley reared and Jason fired his gun into the air.

"Put her down now!" He cocked the gun again.

The revelry ended as suddenly as if a door had slammed. The man with Harriet froze. The other three immediately tossed their hands into the air, which reeked of whiskey. Flustered only for an instant, Harriet kicked free and fell to the ground, just barely managing to land on her feet. Arms pinwheeling, she scrambled for safety, coming to cling to Jason's leg with a death grip.

"What's going on here, boys?" Jason asked calmly. Riley grumbled beneath him, as if demanding an answer as well.

"Mister." The one who had been holding Harriet stepped forward. "Don't think you can just take the girl. She's my property."

"Property?"

"These fools think I'm some mail-order bride named Fiona

from New York." Harriet's face was red as a beet. Sweat glistened on her forehead and her shirt had been ripped open, revealing a camisole. Fear and bile rose up in Jason. If he'd only been a few minutes later, how much worse would this scene have been?

"Pretty strange way to treat a bride," he said coldly.

The man grinned, showing a gap of several teeth. "Well, these fellas helped me pay for her. I was gonna allow a one-time exception to the purity of our marriage vows just for them."

Harriet shivered and tightened her grip on Jason's leg. He understood her revulsion. "This young lady is not a mail-order bride or a prostitute. She's my driver, and she's leaving with me. You can say goodbye and this will all end now"—he drifted his gaze over each of the men—"or I'll be digging graves today." They took too long to answer and Jason pointed the Walker at the groom. "It would behoove you to understand I will do anything to keep her safe. Anything."

Understanding did, indeed, dawn on the man. "I don't think you're bluffing, mister." Slowly, he raised his hands. "Take her and go on."

"I'll be back for my wagon. I expect it to be right where it's at."

———

THEY WERE a good three miles out of Volcano before Jason was convinced the motley crew of forty-niners wasn't coming after them. He shifted in the saddle, almost complained of the death grip Harriet had on him, but thought better of it. She hadn't spoken a word since their departure. Jason was too livid, too torn up over the danger she'd been in, to say anything himself. Wisely, he had just ridden at a slow pace, prayed for her peace, and thanked God for her safety. What if he'd been too late—he pushed the thought and the nausea it caused him away.

Finally, suddenly, Harriet let out a sob that melted some of his anger and fear. Her anguished cry transformed into heaving, messy hiccupping, tearing at his heart. The realization of what had almost happened had hit her with its full force. It had to at some point. Like the first time he'd shot a man. An hour later, he'd thrown up all over the sheriff's desk.

He pulled Riley to a stop in the middle of a large meadow awash in thousands of vibrant wildflowers. A beautiful, peaceful spot. Carefully, he dismounted and then reached for the sobbing mess he called Harriet. He pulled her into a warm embrace, held her close, stroked her head, and whispered reassuring words of peace. Holding her like this filled him with a flood of gratitude. Kissing the top of her head with soul-shaking relief, he thanked God again from the bottom of his heart that she was all right.

But, Lord, this woman is going to kill me. My heart can't take these surprises of hers...

"I-I'm sorry," she whispered. "That's-that's why"—her body and her voice shook—"that's why y-you insisted on t-taking this route."

"I knew it wasn't safe for a woman. Especially you."

He stroked her back for another few minutes and her breathing slowly returned to normal. He could stand here all day holding her but knew Harriet well enough that she would pull herself together.

Sure enough, she did. She burrowed her cheek into his chest one last time, then backed out of his arms. Staring at the ground, she shook her head. "I don't know what's the matter with me. No wonder men think we're the weaker sex. I haven't blubbered like that since I was twelve."

"You shouldn't beat yourself up, Harriet. That was not a good situation. I'm glad I came along when I..." He trailed off, deciding to leave that alone. "Women cry. It's been my experience that men drink too much or throw up. Sometimes they do both."

She hugged herself while her toe pushed a little rock around. "Which do you do?"

"Hmmm." Did he really want to answer that? "I've thrown up...once." And his stomach had lurched madly when he'd seen Harriet with those men. *Lord, it almost stopped my heart.* He'd heard it said love was a bit in your mouth. He'd add, *a hook in your heart.*

"Let's get headed back."

He nodded, mounted, and pulled her up behind him. She clung to him, but more tentatively now. The old Harriet was back in control. What would it take to break through that hard exterior of hers? More disasters? He flinched at the thought.

They rode in silence for a long time, but gradually, Jason began to sense something different in her tension. He couldn't put his finger on it, and the question, *Harriet, what's wrong?* seemed foolish. But he couldn't shake the idea that something else was bothering her, besides nearly being raped.

He heard her swallow, and she spoke. "Jason, there's something I have to tell you. You're not going to like it. And the fact that you're not going to like it...bothers me. I shouldn't care what you think so much...but I do."

He took a deep breath. That was about the most open, most vulnerable thing she'd ever said about their *friendship, partnership,* whatever they had, and it worried him. In fact, he suspected he wasn't going to like what was coming at all. "Say it."

"This morning I agreed to change the contest with Reives. It's winner-take-all now. If we win, we get his horses and wagons, even his cash in the bank. But it's the same thing if he wins."

Stunned, Jason had to take several minutes to roll this news around in his head. Everything? She'd bet him everything? He reined the horse up. "You had no right to do that, Harriet. We had this talk. We're partners." The ember of rage was growing within him. How could she dare make this agreement? Why? "Why did you do this?"

"He came by this morning and offered to buy us out. He knows he's going to lose—"

Jason jumped from the horse and marched several feet away, putting his back to her. He was afraid if he didn't get some distance, he was going to wring her pretty little neck. "That was about the most selfish, underhanded—" He cut himself off. The more he talked, the madder he got. Suddenly though, he cursed and rounded on her. "You almost drowned, Harriet," he yelled, slicing the air with his hand, "because you're so beat up with ambition. It's pretty obvious what those men in Volcano were going to do. And now this? A straight-out betrayal. Damned if you aren't hell-bent on getting yourself killed *and* pushing me away." She flinched each time he cursed and it tweaked his spirit, but he was so angry right now he didn't care what came out of his mouth. "I'm done."

"What?"

"I'm done. I don't know exactly how I'm backing out of this, but I am done. I guess I'll be a silent partner until the race, seeing as how you've bet all my assets."

"But you can't quit." She jumped down and stormed over to him. "I need you to drive the last half of the route."

"I'm done. And I'll tell you another thing. If we weren't still so far from Blessings, I'd leave you here."

"Don't let that stop you. I can walk in."

Jason raised his hands and imagined them around her neck. But instead of grabbing hold of her, he growled and pointed at Riley. "Take your horse. *I'll* walk."

"You said you love me." She whispered it, as if she couldn't believe he'd lied.

"And you think that gives you the right to put your pride, your ambition ahead of everything else?" He leaned closer and spoke through clenched. "It doesn't."

"So, you're abandoning me, too?"

The fact that she saw it that way sliced him, but sometimes, to keep your soul intact, you had to choose a different path. Preferably one that led away from pain and disaster. "I'm letting you go."

CHAPTER TWENTY-SIX

JASON SAT DOWN IN FRONT OF HIS FIREPLACE WITH A CUP OF coffee. He leaned back in the rocking chair and closed his eyes, letting the light and the heat of the fire warm his weary bones. That had been one mighty long walk. Had taken him hours. Hours of slogging, putting one foot in front of the other, walking away from her.

He'd thought leaving her the first time in Sundown had been hard. That had only been a hint of the pain the woman could cause him. He took a sip and sighed. "Lord, I can't imagine she's worth all this..."

His anger had melted away, leaving only an emptiness, a sadness that Jason had never experienced before. How could she be so selfish, so self-centered? As he'd walked, he'd asked that question a million times.

"What am I supposed to do now?"

The answer was immediate. Look for answers in the only place a man could find absolute Truth. He pulled his Bible from the little side table and randomly opened it to 1 Corinthians Chapter 13. As he read it, he sighed. Just opening the Bible to a chapter or verse didn't mean *that* was the word the Lord had for you, but this *was* for him and he knew it.

Charity—meaning here love, being selflessly committed to another—suffered long, was not easily provoked, bore all things, believed all things, hoped all things. It never failed.

Jason had failed Harriet. He had abandoned her. *But, oh, how the woman infuriates me, Lord.*

Yes, a patient voice replied, *she is willful and headstrong. All my children are.*

Jason folded his hands in prayer. *Then show me, Lord, show me how to love her without this pain.*

I know about pain.

Jason could almost imagine a comforting hand coming to rest gently on his shoulder and peace flooded him.

There's always a reason for the hurt I allow. Trust Me and do as I have commanded.

Not the answer he was looking for, but Jason nodded. *Please forgive me, Father, for the things I said and thought. Please help me start over with You and find the strength to forgive her, even if I don't want to be around her.*

My mercies are new every morning, son...

"MR. WINSLET, I need to update you on a few things regarding our contest with Mr. Reives." Harriet settled on a small barrel in front of the man's makeshift desk made humbly of shipping crates and tried to sound more positive than she felt.

"Oh, what's that, young lady?" He settled back and laced slightly arthritic fingers over his abdomen.

"Well, so that everything is clear and we all have the same expectations, I wanted you to know that Mr. Reives and I changed the terms somewhat. You see, we agreed to different stakes. A winner-takes-all competition." The old man's brow dove and she hurried on. "Wagons, horses, cash, and the exclusive right to your shipping contract."

He whistled in astonishment, pondered the ceiling for a second, then came back to her, shaking his head. "Steep terms. And Jason agreed ta this?"

Harriet battled to keep any frustration from her expression. "He's a silent partner. He didn't, um, really have much to say."

"Well..." He trailed off, sounding, she thought, a little perplexed or concerned. "And yer prepared ta take this risk?"

"Mr. Atherton, I will win this contest." *As soon as I find a driver to replace Jason.* "If you're concerned—"

"No." He stroked his beard thoughtfully for a moment. "I reckon it's not my business ta worry 'bout yer business. Seems like a mighty big risk, though." She didn't comment, and he sucked on his cheek for several seconds. "So, what are ya gonna do once ya win this contest and other companies maybe come along and try to open up? Ya gonna keep risking yer company?"

"Mr. Winslet, once I run enough freight for you, no one will doubt my abilities or my company. I'll be able to keep the competition at bay for quite some time. Besides..." She faded off, unsure if she should share her secret ambition. He raised his bushy, silver eyebrows, waiting. "Well, one day, I'd like not only to have my horse ranch back, but I'd like to run a fine resort as well."

"A resort?"

She nodded and smiled sheepishly. "I won't be young forever. The boys can raise the horses. I'll run the hotel and maintain a fine kitchen."

"Yer not plannin' on puttin' my wife out of business, are ya?"

"No, no. The place I have in mind will be much grander,

for longer stays. Families will be able to come and spend the summers." She shrugged. "But one step at a time."

"And yer willing ta risk a dream like that on one race?"

She had doubts, especially since Jason had abandoned her, but neither did she have a choice now. "I'll beat Reives. I have to."

CHAPTER TWENTY-SEVEN

Jason was not ready to see Harriet just yet and ducked around the corner of the mercantile as she was exiting. He wondered if she was shopping or if she had gone to see Mr. Winslet, whose mining office occupied a small room in the back of the store. Her hands were empty, therefore he assumed she'd come to talk business.

Had she told Mr. Winslet about their spat, about the changes to the race, or about losing her *partner*?

Well, the town father needed a few more details before this race went any further, and he intended to share them.

———

Harriet absently swung her reticule around in circles as she crossed Main Street and ambled down a path between the saloon and a lot dotted with tents for *overnighters*. Her thoughts were somber and tangled up over this race. Originally, she had planned for her and Whit to drive the first leg of the route, change the team over at a halfway point where

Jason would then drive on into Truckee. They would reverse things to head back into Blessings.

Now, without Jason...what would they do for another driver? She had prayed he would come to dinner last night, but he hadn't shown. The boys had asked after him but she'd made excuses and let her anger with him spark back to life. He should have never talked to her the way he did. He shouldn't have walked out on their partnership.

The betrayal, the abandonment infuriated her—almost as much as her disappointment that she'd let herself come to care. Frustrated, she scrubbed her face and tried to get her thoughts back on track. Everything they had was riding on this race, and she was down a driver.

She didn't want Whit to drive alone. If something happened, he'd have no help. And this warm weather worried her. A touch of sweat on her upper lip seeded the doubt they might need that second team change more than she'd initially thought. In which case, should she reconsider Devil's Trail? It would require only one team change and save time, too. On the downside, it was more dangerous and would be harder on the animals.

"My, that's a long face."

Harriet looked up into Charly Parkhurst's less-than-handsome face. No, he wasn't good-looking, but his smile was welcoming. "Good morning. What are you doing in Blessings?"

He jerked his thumb toward one of the tents. "Spent the night. Had a shipment for the mine and I got in late." Harriet nodded as Charly joined her on the path. They sauntered along together for a few minutes, slow and a bit aimless. "This town is growing," he said, shoving his hands into his pockets. "I expect you and I will be passing each other on the road more often now."

Maybe, but only if, one, Harriet could take advantage of

Blessing's growth, and two, not lose everything she owned to Reives. Depressed, she sighed.

"So, the long face…" Charly pressed about her mood. "If I ain't being nosy, that is."

"No, no, you're not being nosy." She crossed her arms and sighed heavily again. "That race I was telling you about? My partner was going to drive one leg of it. He backed out."

"Backed out?" Charly seemed offended at the very idea. "Don't sound like much of a partner to me then."

Harriet wanted to sigh again but decided she was waxing maudlin and held it in. "I did something without discussing it with him and he just…and I nearly drowned, and he said he loves me, and he had to rescue me from some trouble in Volacano, and I think I—I think I just drive him crazy," she confessed.

Charly frowned at the nonsensical statements and readjusted his hat over his cropped sweaty hair. They walked in silence for a spell, both lost in thought. "So, your partner is in love with you, but he left," Charly recounted. "You saying that's because he thinks you take too many chances? He doesn't want to stand by and watch you get hurt?"

Harriet toyed with the idea. "I guess that's part of it. The other part is"—it hurt to admit—"I keep cutting him off at the knees, I guess. Making decisions without him."

"Yep, men hate that."

Something about the way he said it made Harriet look up at Charly. It almost sounded as if he were some observer outside the realm of men and women. A disconnected third party. A foolish thought, she shook it off. "Yes, they do. Jason is livid with me. In fact, he's done with me. He wants to get out of our partnership after the race…if I don't lose everything."

"Why? What's the wager?"

Harriet flinched. "Everything. I bet everything. It's winner-take-all."

"Now why did you do that?"

Harriet bit her bottom lip and pondered the question for the millionth time. And she kept coming up with the same answer. "Honestly, for no other reason than he goaded me into it. Because I'm a woman, and that makes me foolish."

Charly cut his eyes at her and regarded her with an and-you-proved-him-right expression.

"I know. I know. I *said* he goaded me into it. But in it I am. *And* down a driver. A darn good one."

Charly sighed and scratched his chin. "When's this race?"

"Day after tomorrow."

"Oh, boy," he whispered and scratched his head. "Okay." He said it again, louder. "Okay. I'll drive for ya. And you'll win. And then you work things out with your partner."

Harriet stopped and turned to him. "You're a *good* driver?"

Charly chuckled but it turned into an all-out guffaw. "Yeah." He slapped a hand on her shoulder. "Little miss, you just drop my name in front of Reives and watch his expression." Before Harriet could respond, Charly's gaze shot past her and he slapped his thigh with obvious delight. "Speak of the devil." He grabbed Harriet's hand and dragged her across the street, dodging wagons, horses, men, and mules.

"Reives," Charly yelled.

The man, about to step inside the mercantile, halted and spun toward the voice. At first, he smiled, until a glance showed Harriet in tow. His friendly humor melted off his face. "Parkhurst." He paused as they stepped up on the boardwalk and then nodded at Harriet. "Mrs. Pullen."

"Reives, Mrs. Pullen here wants to know if I'm a good driver."

Reives's eyes narrowed with suspicion. "You decide to drive for me?"

"Nope. I'm gonna drive for the lady here."

Reives's face hardened like plaster drying in the sun. "Whatever she's paying you, I'll double it."

Harriet's mouth nearly fell open, but she managed to stop it in time. Charly merely chuckled. "No thanks." He slapped Reives on the shoulder so hard the slender man's feet shifted to keep him upright. "See ya on the trail."

Reives dragged his gaze over the two and then nodded at Charly. "Well, may the best man win."

Charly's lips tightened, but neither he nor Harriet said anything as Reives slipped inside the store.

CHAPTER TWENTY-EIGHT

HARRIET HAD ONLY JUST RETURNED FROM A TRIP TO DUTCH Creek when Wyatt told her Mr. Winslet wanted to see her. A little puzzled, she stripped off her gloves and handed them to her son. "Rub the horses down good. I'll meet you and your brother at the Winslet House for dinner. I'm too tired to cook."

His blue eyes brightened. "Yes, ma'am."

She pinched him lightly on one of his adorable, round cheeks and trudged off to see Mr. Winslet.

She was surprised to see Reives had been summoned as well.

"Please, Mrs. Pullen, have a seat." The old man motioned to a box in front of his desk. She sat down, followed by Mr. Winslet, but Reives remained standing, as if he was in a hurry to leave. "I've been givin' this some thought," the mine owner continued, "I have decided there should be a little change to yer contest."

Harriet and Reives exchanged wary glances with each other and Mr. Winslet.

Reives leaned forward and laid a hand on the man's desk. "What kind of change?"

Mr. Winslet pulled a pocket watch from his vest and laid it on the desk. "I've decided there won't be a race. At least not ya two directly against each other. I'm going to time ya. Yer going to leave Blessings three hours apart, deliver the freight in Truckee, return here empty. Fastest time wins. *Not* the first one to cross the finish line."

Both Harriet and Reives balked in protest, but she managed to formulate a coherent question first. "Why are you making this change?"

"Safety." The old man grinned so broadly his wiry white beard doubled the width of his face. "I have it on good authority ya two might do just about anythin' to win. We do it this way, ya won't really know if yer ahead or behind. Should keep ya safer. Should keep yer horses safer."

Harriet grudgingly agreed with the reasoning, but she had so looked forward to leaving Reives in her dust. Scowling, Reives paced the small office. "Forgive me, Mr. Winslet, but the lady and I had agreed on terms for this contest. First one to cross the finish line. A head-to-head race. I don't think I'm comfortable changing things now."

Mr. Winslet tilted his head to one side. "Ya want a shot at my business, you'll do this one thing my way."

Reives debated a moment but finally nodded. "All right. Anything else?"

"No, I reckon the rest of yer rules'll be just fine. No more than two team changes. Two wagons of equal weight. Same freight. You'll start here and finish here. Pete and me will see ya off and be waitin' to enter yer time on yer return."

Tension writhed in the air, but Harriet wouldn't deny a sense of exhilaration as well. Finally, she would prove what her horses could do. If only Jason hadn't—no, if *she* hadn't abused their partnership. Their friendship.

Mr. Winslet nodded. "All right then. Reives, I'll see ya here at six. Mrs. Pullen, nine sharp." She rose and the mine owner came with her. "By the way, my lumbago says there's rain a-comin'. Take yer slickers."

CHAPTER TWENTY-NINE

JASON FINISHED CHECKING ON A FEW DETAILS FOR THE RACE, then swung back by the office. Somehow, he and Harriet had avoided each other for two days and she wasn't there again. He'd hoped to make it look as if bumping into each was unavoidable, but apparently God wasn't going to make this easy.

Jason did owe her an apology. He had made the choice to forgive her, whether she wanted or even thought she needed his forgiveness. Beyond that, he just wasn't sure how much more knife-twisting he could take. Being around her, especially if she was going to keep making bad choices and, frankly, trying to wear the pants in this partnership—well, it was just going to be too hard.

Resigned, he rode on out to her place. Whit was out front chopping wood. Wyatt was oiling the new tack. They greeted Jason with warm smiles that reminded him how much he missed their company.

"Ma's in the house." Whit set a log on the chopping block and grinned. "She sure has been grumpy the last couple of days."

Jason flung his reins around the porch rail and stomped across the wood. "She's not the only one."

The door was open and he was about to call out when Harriet came out from behind her bedroom curtain—buttoning a pair of pants.

"Whit, what do you th—?"

She froze when her eyes landed on Jason. For a moment, he froze as well, but then remembered his hat and slid it off.

Pants. She's wearing pants. His shock must have shown on his face.

Her quick flash of what he interpreted as happiness faded. She fluffed the loose legs and plucked at the pleated waist. "I take it you don't approve."

When had she cared what he thought? But he hadn't come for a fight. "I think—I think..." *The men in town will howl like coyotes.* "I understand why you're wearing them. For the race. Just the race." Not a question, more of a strong suggestion and he regretted his tone instantly.

Her face tightened and she flung her braid over her shoulder. "I need to be able to move. My skirt keeps getting caught on the brake handle."

He pursed his lips and nodded. Just seeing her affected him. What he wouldn't give if he could take her in his arms and kiss away this stubborn, pig-headed streak of hers. "I'd rather you be safe. Pants make sense. The men won't understand. Doubt the women in town will either."

Her face fell. Her jade eyes darkened with acceptance. "It's not fair."

"No, I reckon it's not." He twirled his hat for a moment. "I didn't come to talk about pants. Harriet"—he glanced over his shoulder, Whit was still chopping wood—"I came to apologize."

She turned and drifted over to the stove. "You shouldn't have talked to me like that."

"I—" He stared up at the ceiling, praying the right words would fall from heaven. "I was out of line. I shouldn't have lost my temper. I shouldn't have cursed." He paused and she lifted her head. He knew she was waiting for the last apology. He couldn't oblige. "But what I said about being partners still stands, Harriet. I can't watch you—I can't be party to your foolishness. If you won't listen to me..." He had to take a moment to control the tightening in his throat.

She whirled on him. "You mean if I won't do what you tell me?" She said it softly, but with venom.

Disappointed, downright sick this wasn't going well, Jason shook his head. "It's not like that. Partners talk about things. They value what the other brings to the table. Far as I can see, you just hold the sins of a husband against me."

She paled but didn't say anything. Jason nodded and dropped his hat in place. "Good luck tomorrow."

———

THE SOFT KNOCK on the office door alerted Jason instantly. It had the sound of something clandestine. Just bending down to stoke the fire, he glanced at the entrance. A handful of people had been tasked with keeping an eye on Harriet and Reives. If word had leaked they were watching the man, then no telling who could be on the other side of that door. It *should* be a friend. Just in case, though, Jason reached for the gun belt hanging from his office chair and slid the Colt from the holster. "Who is it?" he asked, cocking it.

"It's Michael."

He released the hammer and opened the door. Michael worked security at the mine. He and Pete Jones, the head security officer, were extra eyes for Jason. A fair-haired young man with hazel eyes, the Southerner was fairly new in town, but Pete had sworn by him.

"Come on in, Michael."

The young man looked around questioningly.

"No shipping today. We're resting the horses." Still, he had expected to see Harriet this morning. "You can talk freely."

"I followed Reives's driver. They're gonna take a tough route." His Southern lilt had a way of softening the serious information. "I'd say it's high risk."

"Which way are they going?"

"Devil's Tail."

Jason's brow rose. Yet, the news bode well for Harriet. "That's pretty foolish." Jason had talked her out of using the trail a week earlier. She was going to take Hangin' Dog. Tough, steep, one river crossing, but not as unpredictable and narrow as Devil's Tail. "I doubt they'll pull it off. Reives thinks the shorter length of the trail is worth the risk. He's wrong. Do you know the drivers?"

"They came in with the horses."

"From Texas then," Jason surmised.

"Also, they already have four horses waiting at a halfway point."

Jason frowned. "That was smart. They'll be plenty rested tomorrow."

"That's what I thought."

"Well." Jason shrugged. "I told Harriet it wouldn't be a cakewalk. Are you ready for tomorrow?"

Michael nodded but then scratched the small scar on his chin thoughtfully. "What if they make it? Their time will be very good."

"If they make it up and back on Devil's Tail, they deserve to win."

———

A FULL MOON cast the corral in a magical, silvery mix of light and shadow. Enough light for Harriet, her boys, and Charly to cut out the four horses for the second leg of the race. They worked quickly and quietly, putting the animals in halters and tying them to a lead line attached to Charly's mount Venus and Wyatt's horse Mustang.

"All right." Harriet patted the horses on their rear ends as Charly and Wyatt swung up into the saddles. "Whit and I leave at nine. We'll be along as fast as we can." She shifted over to Wyatt, clutching his knee. "Do everything Charly tells you, and do it quick. You hear me?"

"Yes, ma'am."

She stepped back and nodded at Charly. "We should be there around noon. Faster if we can."

"We'll be ready. 'Member what I said about your ambition."

"I'll remember." She might ignore it, but she'd remember. Regardless, she prayed for safety for them all as the pair headed off into the shadowy landscape.

"I wish we would have been smart enough to get the horses out on the trail as early as Reives did." Whit sounded frustrated at the lapse.

"We needed you and your brother here driving, Whit. We couldn't spare you. But it doesn't matter. Our horses will be rested enough."

She crossed her arms and watched until Charly and Wyatt disappeared over a hill. Suddenly she felt so lonely and afraid, crushed by all this responsibility and the weight of the stakes. How had she come to do this without Jason?

Was she punishing him for Henry's sins? Was she terrified of letting any man close to her again? She supposed there was some truth to that. Oh, if she'd only swallowed her pride a little.

She would. *After* the race. After they won, she would sit down with Jason, apologize, and promise to be more respectful, more trusting. As soon as she had Winslet's freight contract in her hand. She needed that little bit of security. Then she would make amends of some sort with Jason.

THE NEXT MORNING, five hundred pounds of freight was loaded into the back of Harriet's wagon. Much to her annoyance, Reives was there to watch, as if she might cheat. Still, since he wasn't a driver, he'd had to pass the duty to a professional. His fate was out of his hands and she did not envy him. Sitting around waiting and watching would have killed her.

She and Whit waited quietly as Mr. Winslet and his security officer, Peter Jones, inspected the wagon. Recalling the cut reins from a week ago, she hoped they did a thorough inspection. She and Whit had gone over the wagon with a fine-toothed comb at daybreak. They had not let the wagon or the horses out of their sight since.

"Everything looks all right," Pete said, backing away from the wagon.

"I'm satisfied," Mr. Winslet said, pulling his pocket watch from his vest. "Ya ready, Mrs. Pullen?"

She looked at Whit, who was holding the reins. He nodded, and she smiled at her handsome young son. Almost as full of fire and ambition as Harriet. "We're ready."

Mr. Winslet raised his hand and popped open the watch. "Aaaaand, go!" He dropped his hand, Whit slapped the reins, and they were off.

AN HOUR AND A HALF LATER, they met up with Charly and Wyatt and hitched up the fresh team. Being the more experienced drivers, Charly and Harriet went on, with strict orders for the boys to wait and tend to the horses. The weather was warm, but not overly so, and the sky above was a stunning azure filled with fluffy popcorn clouds.

Beside her, Charly drove with intent focus. His face settled into a mask of grim determination and he didn't dally with chitchat. He kept the horses at a steady but hard pace.

Harriet had ridden this route twice, once with Whit and once again with Jason. It sloped down out of the mountains at a mostly gentle pace. There was one creek to cross, and then once they were down to the valley, they would cross the shallow Donner Creek and be in Truckee.

Headed downhill now through a forest of tall lodgepole pines, Harriet figured the horses should be in pretty good shape to come back up, but she wouldn't be able to push them at this speed. Charly was laying the foundation for a strong lead on the clock. All Harriet had to do was not mess it up when it was her turn to drive.

"We're making good time." Harriet had to shout over the rumble of the wagon and the pounding hooves of the team. She would have given anything for the driver beside her to be Jason.

Charly nodded and flicked the long reins. "I think it'll be your race to lose."

Lord, please, help us keep up the pace.

CHAPTER THIRTY

THE SIGHT OF REIVES'S WAGON SITTING IN A GULLY, ONE WHEEL lying off to the side while the two drivers did repairs, pleased Jason to no end. Peering through the branches of a cedar, he watched the two men jump from the wagon to deal with the delay.

The accident coming down the steepest part of the Devil's Tail would no doubt take a toll on their time. If there had been a lead, it was evaporating quickly.

One of the drivers cursed, threw down a jack handle, and pulled a revolver from his holster. He aimed it at the sky and fired. Jason tilted his head, puzzled. A moment later, a faint answering report cleared up his confusion.

A signal.

He mulled over the implication. Admitting defeat? Announcing a delay?

Or maybe...

An alarming thought struck him. If Reives's team wanted to stay in this race, Harriet would have to be delayed, too...if not knocked out altogether. And, clearly, there was someone out there waiting in case of a signal. Someone capable of sabotaging Harriet's team? Michael was supposed to be watching them, but he needed to be warned.

His heart jolting, Jason clutched the Colt on his hip, wheeled around, and raced back up the steep mountainside to retrieve his horse.

HARRIET INCLINED HER HEAD SLIGHTLY. The wagon, empty now, was leaner and less of a drag on the horses, but it was still a noisy ride. She could have sworn, though, she'd heard— or more like, felt—thunder? The concussion of thunder. The sky over the valley was still clear, except for the light and airy summer clouds.

"Did you hear anything?"

"What's that?" Charly inclined an ear.

"Did you hear anything a second ago?"

Charly shook his head. Harriet looked ahead, where the road turned north and headed back into the mountains. The noise had come from up there. *If* she'd heard anything at all.

Charly leaned over. "Push 'em a little harder. The wagon's empty. In less than ten miles, we'll change 'em out. They'll be all right."

Harriet agreed and slapped the reins across the geldings' backs. Just a little more speed might make all the difference.

The road began its climb and the air cooled. The scent of pine wafted over them. Harriet loosened the reins and let the animals slow a little. She was into a rhythm. The horses were in perfect time with one another. The wagon was flying along and she was feeling that this contest truly was hers to lose.

And she wouldn't.

A few miles in, they rounded a curve and she snatched the horses to a skidding stop. The road ahead was covered by a mammoth mass of rubble that swept across it and spilled down the steep side several hundred feet.

"Well, look at that," Charly whispered from beside her.

"A slide?"

"Looks like." But Harriet thought his voice was strange, as if he was awed...or suspicious. Charly climbed down and approached the mess of rocks, trees, and dirt. Harriet set the brake and followed suit. Thumbs hooked on his belt loop, her driver shook his head. "I don't like this."

Slides happened all the time in the mountains. They weren't rare by any means. But here, now? Harriet wondered if her suspicion bordered on paranoia.

"Well, we're not going over it." Charly ambled to the edge and looked down the long, steep bank. Shale slithered out from under his feet and he stepped back. "And we're not going around it."

They could go back and get men to clear it, which would take hours, and the contest would be lost. Or they could go back two miles and take the cutoff to Devil's Tail.

Charly silently scanned their surroundings again, his cold gaze sending chills up Harriet's arms. He didn't like this, that was obvious.

"You don't think this was an accident, do you?"

"No, I don't." He pulled his revolver from its holster, spun the cylinder, apparently to make sure all the chambers were loaded, and slid it back into its home. "I know you know the options. What do you want to do?"

Oh, God, she pleaded, wiping sweat off her brow. *What do You want us to do? I can't lose everything again. Not again...*

She swallowed her fear. Or tried to. "The Devil's Tail. It'll be hard on the horses, but I don't know what choice we have."

CHAPTER THIRTY-ONE

JASON THUNDERED THROUGH THE MOUNTAINS, TAKING SOME pretty sketchy trails to cross over from Devil's Tail to Hangin' Dog. He pushed Dollar too hard at one point, down a steep mountainside and up the other, but he kept hearing those gunshots in his head. Signals to put something in motion.

Suddenly he burst out onto the trail and reined in, spinning Dollar in a slow circle while he got his bearings. Confident he knew his location on Hangin' Dog, he spurred the horse and took off again. A few miles down, the trail opened up into a fine pasture, the halfway point. He found the boys there. Whit and Wyatt had the horses tied to a picket line and were sitting in the shade, chewing on grass. When they saw Jason, they jumped to their feet and waved.

Jason waved back and trotted on in. He didn't wish to alarm the boys, but clearly, Harriet and Charly hadn't made it in yet. "Any sign of your ma yet?" he asked, riding up to them.

"No." Whit shook his head. "And I'm starting to worry."

"Yeah." Jason backed Dollar up. "They're liable to show up in a hurry, so be ready. I'll go see where they are."

Without waiting for a response, he spurred Dollar and put the horse in a full gallop.

JASON JERKED Dollar to a stop and stared at the mess in the road. A major slide blocked Hangin' Dog to the point it would take weeks to dig this mess out. A mammoth movement of trees, earth, and boulders had nearly rearranged half the mountain.

Slides weren't uncommon, but this one launched a sick feeling in his gut. He just didn't believe it was an accident. He looked to his left, down the steep mountainside. Debris, loose shale, and the hard angle would have made getting around this from the other side impossible. He wouldn't risk Dollar in that shale, either. He glanced up the mountainside. Steeper, rockier, dotted with trees.

No good choices. But he had to get to the other side. He dismounted and walked the horse up the mountain, at times the two of them scrambling like cats to keep their footing. *Please, Lord, let her be all right. Help me to get to the other side.*

Both he and Dollar broke into a sweat climbing up and then over to the other side of the slide. Sometimes the shale drifted underneath their feet like water, other times, gravel and bigger rocks gave way. Jason grabbed every sapling and cedar branch he could get his hands on to anchor him. Dollar plugged away behind him, seemingly understanding the urgency of this trek.

Finally, they made it to the other side. Harriet's tracks were obvious. They'd ridden up to the edge of the slide. Two sets of tracks said she and Charly had walked about, probably debating, then they had decided to turn around.

Jason knew the only choice they had was to go back two

miles to where Hangin' Dog and Devil's Tail crossed. She was going to take the other trail home.

Shale and gravel streamed down in a small rivulet and Jason pulled his gun. Movement? Had he seen movement in the trees? A shadow of a man, high above him?

Charly?

"Jason," a voice hailed from on high.

Michael. "Yo, down here."

On foot, Michael was carefully navigating his way down to the trail. Stepping, sliding, clinging to saplings, he worked his way to Jason. "This was no accident." He jumped the last two feet onto the trail and pointed to the slide. "Somebody blew it."

"What makes you so sure?" He wanted Michael to be wrong.

"I found this."

He reached out and handed Jason a palm-sized tin, bright yellow and round. *Hercules No. 6 Blasting Caps* was stamped on the outside. He lifted the lid. The tin was empty. The sick feeling in the pit of his stomach grew. "Where are Charly and Harriet?" For the first time, the fear struck him that they were buried underneath a ton of rock and someone had taken the wagon.

"I was following them like you asked, then I saw somebody trailing us. I went after him. When the dynamite blew, it spooked my horse and threw me. By the time I had him gathered up, you were coming in from the other side."

Jason nudged Dollar and he studied the ground again. The only tracks here belonged to Harriet and Charly. "Michael, you've got your horse?"

"Yes. He's tied up there."

"All right. You get him and head back to Blessings. Tell Mr. Winslet and Pete somebody is purposely driving Harriet toward Devil's Tail. He doesn't declare a winner, doesn't award any contract, until we find her and clear up what's going on. You understand?"

Michael was already scrambling up the hill. "And we'll bring back help."

"Fine." Jason started to spur Dollar, but something else occurred to him. "Michael, if Reives—or whoever—did this, they may be on their way back to Blessings. Keep your eyes open."

CHAPTER THIRTY-TWO

The rain burst from a sky that Jason would have sworn was clear and blue only moments before. Regardless, it fell with violence and intensity. Thunder and lightning crashed, and still, he kept Dollar moving at a hard gallop.

The trail, growing muddier and more treacherous by the second, turned down at a steep angle. It zig-zagged down the mountain, hairpin curves, and switchbacks slowing Dollar's speed. Small, rushing waterfalls poured off the mountain, cascading across his path. Finally, the road straightened and made a long plunge toward a creek.

Through the driving rain, he saw movement several hundred yards up. A flash of lightning illuminated Harriet slipping into her pommel slicker. He yelled, but the weather drowned him out. Dollar picked up his speed on his own and raced toward his owner.

To Jason's consternation, Charly appeared to be veering off the road and heading for the creek. As he drew closer, though, he could see the cause for the change of course. The bridge over the creek was *gone*. Nothing remained but a skeletal, tangled base. It had been blown to smithereens.

"Harriet," he yelled again, racing to join them.

———

HARRIET COULD HAVE CRIED. In fact, she probably was, but the pouring rain that had happened as suddenly as a bursting bladder washed away her tears. The jagged, skeletal remains of the bridge left no doubt this contest had been sabotaged. Someone had blown it to bits to keep her trapped here.

Beside her, Charly cursed.

No, no, no, Harriet screamed in her head. *We can't let it end like this. I won't. Oh, God, please show me—*

The remains of the bridge sat in a low, wide creek. It wasn't fifty yards from shore to shore, and there was a small, oblong island in the middle. The bank was a little steep on the other side, but they could do this. People had crossed here before there was a bridge, based on older tracks and a depression in the bank. She handed Charly the reins and yelled over the rain, "We'll cross the creek. I'm going to get my slicker before I drown."

Charly, who had smelled the rain coming, had already put on his slicker. He backed the wagon up a few feet while Harriet fished out her coat from the box beneath their bench. She'd lost her hat several miles back and would give a hundred dollars for one right now. Cold water drenched her hair, poured into her mouth and eyes, and down her back.

She blinked crazily, trying to keep her vision clear. They'd conquered the steepest part of the Devil's Tail. The rest of the route wasn't as steep. Once they crossed the water they could make up some time. They would have to push the horses harder than she'd like, but she wasn't done yet. If Mr. Reives thought blowing up a bridge was going to stop her, he'd taken leave of his senses.

Carefully, Charly guided the horses to the water's edge.

The creek was almost lazy here, Harriet noted. The current was slow but picking up, and the bottom was mostly gravel, littered here and there with a few boulders.

To her left, the bones of the bridge pointed skyward like dangerous, jagged toothpicks. Oh, she couldn't wait to see Reives's face when they showed up in Blessings before his team. She and Charly and these fine geldings were going to make quick work of this creek and race by his wagon like it was standing still—

The water was higher.

A moment ago, it had barely swirled around the horse's knees. Now it was touching their bellies. Unease wiggled in her gut.

"We're going back," Charly announced, pulling the reins to the right.

"What?" Harriet screamed over the rain.

"Flash flood. We're getting back on dry land."

"What? No," Harriet raged. She grabbed the reins from him. "We're crossing. We can beat the water."

"You should think about your boys, Harriet. You keep going they're not gonna have a mother."

"I'm not turning back." Fury exploded in her. "I didn't think you were a coward, Charly."

"I'm no coward, but neither am I stupid. Now turn this thing around."

"I won't." Harriet slapped the reins, urging the horses on. The water had risen another three inches at least.

"Fine. I'm not dying with you." Charly leaped from the wagon and headed back to shore, wading, almost swimming, the water was rising so fast. Lightning flashed and thunder reverberated in the canyon like the voice of God.

CHAPTER THIRTY-THREE

HARRIET SHOOK OFF HER SHOCK AT CHARLY'S BETRAYAL AS THE wagon fish-tailed. The horses whinnied, their eyes rolling with fear. The water had reached their chests now. *The island. If we can get to the island, it'll be easier from there.* "Yaaah!" She slapped the reins, the wet leather making a sharp cracking sound. "Come on, boys!"

"No, Harriet!" From nowhere, Jason materialized and swept her out of the wagon.

At first, she was too stunned to react, but as he lifted her and pulled her out of the wagon, she screamed and flailed and clung to the reins. "No! Let me cross!"

"You're going to drown, Harriet. It's a flash flood!"

Jason threw her across his saddle violently and turned Dollar back toward the shore. The horse struggled against the current. Harriet raged like a trapped cougar, kicking, screaming, writhing in the saddle. "My horses," she railed. She twisted in time to see them reach the island, which was already being swallowed by the rising water.

"They're not important, Harriet."

Dollar bucked and swam, ice-cold water flooded inside Harriet's slicker. Then Dollar's feet found solid purchase, and he leaped from the water. He lunged for the high ground, climbing, climbing until they stood on the road near the destroyed bridge. Livid, Harriet kicked free of Jason and ran to the edge of it so she could see her horses. Axton and Doc stood confused on the island, the water swirling around their pasterns. She watched in misery as it climbed to their knees and to their bellies.

Sensing the danger, the horses pranced, whinnied, tossed their heads. As if of one mind, they shuddered and then leaped into the water, headed for the opposite shore. For an instant, they both disappeared and Harriet screamed.

Her horses. Her beautiful horses—

They reemerged, pawing, splashing, screaming with fear. The wagon tipped behind them, twisted violently, then broke free and the water took it. Unhitched from their burden, the horses clambered for dry land. The creek was a raging torrent now, deafening in its force. Great tree trunks rushed by like mammoth ships.

Go, boys, go. Please, God, let them live....

Axton and Doc scrambled out of the water, up the bank, still hitched together but dragging their reins, the harness pole hanging in two. Another flash of lightning and Harriet saw them making for the road like the hounds of hell were after them.

But they were safe. She was safe. And she'd lost everything. Again.

Her knees buckled and she collapsed. Defeated. Broken. Oh, so weary. In an instant, Jason was beside her, holding her, kissing her, whispering her name in her ear. Despair gave way to a glimmer of joy as rain and tears filled her eyes. She was alive. Twice, God had sent someone to save her. *Twice.* And Jason...Jason was here.

He was here. He was real.

She pulled back and touched his face beneath his hat. He was here. The fear, the relief she saw in his wide, blue eyes tore something loose in her. She tried to speak, but the words couldn't get past the knot in her throat.

"Harriet." He clasped her face, rain streaming in her eyes, down her cheeks and over his hands. "Harriet, it's all right, it's all right. You're alive. And your boys, they're safe. That's all that matters." He was talking at a crazy speed, as if he was desperate to say it all before time ran out—or she quit listening. "I'll make sure you don't lose them. We'll think of something. Somehow, we'll get the wagon and—"

"No, no, no," she cried, shaking her head. Tears choked her voice as she tried to yell over the roar of the rain and the creek. "I don't care. I don't care. I'm sorry, Jason. I'm so sorry. If I have you and my children, that's all I'll ever need." He stared at her with a gaze so full of love and relief that he nearly stopped her heart. And as if the universe wanted to hear her confession, the storm retreated to a gentle shower. Harriet clutched Jason's cheeks and spoke softly. "That's all I'll ever need."

He kissed her and then held her as tight as a man saving a drowning victim. "I thought I was going to lose you," he whispered against her lips.

He pulled her to her feet and she clung to him, desperate to never let him go. "Oh, I've been so blind." She pressed her forehead to his chest. "So cruel. And stupid. Forgive me. Please. Please."

He was quiet for a moment, then he tilted her chin up. "You are willful and headstrong, Harriet Pullen. And yet I cannot help but love you." She smiled with hope and he smiled back.

"Will you—will you." She wiped water from her face and tried again. "Promise me you'll never leave me again." He kissed her, lovingly, tenderly, and Harriet wanted to weep with joy and shame at the same time. *How could I have been so fooolish, blind, and just plain stupid, stupid, stupid?*

"Harriet," he whispered against her lips, "Truth is, I never left you in the first place."

CHAPTER THIRTY-FOUR

IT TOOK HOURS BETWEEN WAITING FOR THE CREEK TO DROP AND gathering up horses. Still, Harriet, Jason, the boys, Charly, and the handful of men Michael had rounded up finally made it back to Blessings around midnight.

Harriet didn't think she had one ounce of energy left. Assuming the shipping contract had been awarded to Reives and just too tired to care, she climbed down from the wagon and fell into Jason's waiting arms.

"Tired, huh?"

"All I want to do is sleep, but then I know we have to get up tomorrow morning and sign it all over to Reives." She clutched his shirt and buried her face in his chest, wishing she could hide from the world. "I'm so sorry. This is all my fault. I've cost you so much, but..."

"But what?"

She took a deep breath and looked into his eyes. "I've lost so much, but at least now I know what I've *gained*. And it makes what I lost trivial. I'll tell you something else I was thinking."

"What's that?"

He stroked her cheek, and for a moment, she lost her train of thought. His expression was so serene, so peaceful. "I, um... the river." She wanted to say this without crying, but her throat tightened. "If Charly hadn't been there the first time to fish me out—I think I would have drowned. And that didn't wake me up. The second time, you saved me." Harriet's chin quivered, and for a moment, she couldn't speak. Her eyes burned from the pooling tears. "I see now how stubborn and foolish I was, and He...showed me such grace." Overcome with gratitude, she buried her head in his chest again and wept. "He gave me a second chance."

Jason hugged her and sighed, the most pure sound of contentment Harriet had ever heard. "I tried so hard to give up on you," he whispered, "and He just wouldn't let me."

He ran his hand up and down her back slowly, gently. A simple touch, and yet it created such joy in her, filled her with hope for the future—and not one built on unbridled bitterness.

"You have been an expensive venture, but"—he kissed the top of her head—"I think I came out all right, too."

"Maybe better than ya think, son."

Jason and Harriet pulled themselves from the moment to see Mr. Winslet coming toward them, swinging a lantern. "Been waitin' all night for ya folks ta get back."

Holding tight to Jason, Harriet prepared herself for the inevitable decision, though she didn't think it was fair. Reives was certainly the one who would benefit from sabotaging her, but without proof, what could they do? Right now, she was simply too tired to care. Besides, considering what she'd gained today, the shipping company was a moth-eaten ruin.

"When Michael came back to get ya some help," Mr. Winslet continued, "he told us what happened on the trail. Pete went and had a little talk with Reives. Seems durin' the discussion, the man sort of accidentally spilled his saddle bag and—wouldn't ya know—some blastin' caps spilled out. Careless." Mr. Winslet *tsked* and shook his head. "And awfully coincidental. So, Pete told him to sit tight and we'd sort all this out in the mornin'. Seems Mr. Reives didn't want ta wait." Silence from Jason and Harriet prompted him to add, "Oh, he skedaddled with his horses."

Hope was building in Harriet and she could feel Jason's heart beating beneath her fingers. "Are you saying, Mr. Winslet, that we won?" She was almost afraid to hope. "That we get your shipping contract?"

"Well, I don't know what you've *won*. Like I said, he took his horses. Don't know 'bout any other assets yer entitled ta, based on the terms of yer wager, but, yes, at least ya do get my shipping business."

Harriet looked up at Jason. "Oh, we won something, Mr. Winslet. Trust me. We won."

"Good. If yer satisfied, I'm satisfied. Pete'll ride out after Reives if ya folks think there's charges to be filed."

Jason's good humor evaporated from his expression. "Harriet, I think we should. Reives upped his game with cutting your reins and using dynamite. He's liable to hurt somebody. And there are Kansas warrants out on him. I can make sure he goes to jail for something."

"All right then."

"All right then," Mr. Winslet repeated. "I'll make sure Pete fetches him back."

"I am curious, though." Harriet tilted her head questioningly at the old gentleman. "Did Reives's wagon make it in? Did they post a time?"

"Five hours, fourteen minutes, and thirty-two seconds."

Harriet chuckled and let it blossom into a laugh that refreshed her soul, especially when Jason joined in. She leaped into his arms and hugged him with abandon. "We would have beat him. We would have beat him."

"Dang straight, we would have," Jason agreed, hugging her back.

Frowning playfully, Charly walked up and shoved his hat back an inch, waiting for the laughter to fade. When the couple separated, he rested an elbow on Harriet's shoulder. "You know what you're getting into with this one, Jason? She's 'bout crazy."

Jason grinned, his teeth gleaming in the moonlight. "I believe I can bear it."

"She's all yours then. I know *I'm* never gettin' in another wagon with her. *Especially* if there's a creek nearby." Charly winked at Harriet and strode off to get his horse, their laughter filling the night air in Blessings once more.

EPILOGUE

"The blindfold is a bit tedious, Jason."

From the back of the wagon, Whit, Wyatt, and Katie chuckled at their mother's comment like little girls with a secret. Harriet was not amused, though it pleased her beyond words to finally have her daughter with them. "How much longer?"

"We're almost there. Another minute."

Harriet sighed heavily and held on to Jason. Riding blindfolded in this bumpy wagon for almost an hour was making her irritable. And they had so much work back at the office. She didn't have time for this silliness.

"All right." Jason must have pulled the reins because Harriet felt the wagon come to a stop. "Whit, Wyatt, Katie, you know where to stand." The wagon dipped and rebounded noticeably as her children leaped free of it. "Sit tight, Harriet, I'm coming." Again the wagon jostled, and a moment later, she felt Jason's strong arms lift her from the seat and set her on the ground.

"Tell me this," she asked as he spun her around. "Am I going to like this surprise?"

"Oh, I think so."

Holding her shoulders, he guided her carefully over slightly uneven ground. Harriet smelled the scent of grass and pine. She might have even caught the sound of a cow mooing in the distance? What in the world—?

Jason untied the blindfold. "Take a look."

The cloth fell away from her eyes. She blinked to bring things into focus beneath the late afternoon sun. They were all standing in a huge, flower-dotted meadow of at least a dozen acres. It sloped down and turned into a rolling, green valley that drifted all the way to the foot of the Sierras several miles distant.

Then Harriet noticed the woman off to their right. A lovely, young, Hispanic girl with an olive complexion and warm brown eyes. She was wearing a brightly colored dress, at least a dozen bracelets, and holding a large, blank canvas. Harriet had seen the woman around town recently. And she was always sketching something.

"Harriet, this is Araceli Arroyo. I have engaged her to paint a family portrait of us."

Harriet gasped with delight. Oh, how she loved this man. "Jason, that's a wonderful idea. Ms. Arroyo, I'm so excited. Thank you for doing this."

The young lady smiled and dipped her chin. "It is my pleasure."

"I felt it was important to capture this day." Jason took Harriet by the elbow and led her to where the children were standing shoulder-to-shoulder.

"And what day would that be?" Their wedding anniversary wasn't for another month. Had she forgotten Jason's birthday? No, that was in the fall.

Grinning like a mule eating briers, he pulled a document from his breast pocket and waved it at Harriet. "We are the proud owners, Harriet, of four thousand prime acres. Welcome to your new horse ranch and, eventually, resort."

Harriet's hand flew to her mouth. Instantly, tears filled her eyes and made their escape down her cheeks. The boys stepped apart to reveal a stake in the ground. "That," Katie said, "is a corner stake for our new house. Finally, I get my own room."

Harriet was speechless. From behind her, Jason slipped his arms around her waist and nodded at the horizon. "We got in one shipment of cattle. A hundred head. I'll let you buy the horses. And when you're ready to build your resort, Harriet, there's a lake out there. Twenty-six acres of water."

She could see it. She could see a fine place families would come to and spend their summers together. They would come back year after year and then when the families grew, grand-children would come along.

She spun round to him and cupped his cheek. Whit and Wyatt rolled their eyes and looked away. Katie gazed on with an awed expression like a girl dying to be in love.

"Here they go," Whit whined. Katie smacked him in the stomach.

Harriet ignored them. "When I came here, I was so bitter and I wanted to do all this on my own." She kissed Jason on the mouth tenderly, longingly. "You and the Lord have been so patient with me. Thank you for suffering through till I came to my senses."

He dipped his head and gave her a crooked little smile. "I knew you'd be worth the wait." He frowned. "Well, I was pretty sure."

DEAR READER, I hope you enjoyed reading my fictional version of the real Harriet Pullen's life. She was a pistol. If you enjoyed the story, I truly, deeply, sincerely would appreciate a review. I say it all the time, but those things make the famous —or infamous—algorithms of the retailers like an author. So, the more, the better. And thank you.

Harriet Pullen was a real-life character. "Abandoned and nearly bankrupted by her husband, Harriet Pullen pulled herself up by her bootstraps and vowed to make a living somehow. To get started, she placed her four children with friends in Seattle and headed north to Alaska to look for work. Her desperation for employment must have shown on her face because only moments after making it to the beach, a man tapped her on the shoulder and asked her if she could cook..." If you'd like to learn more about the *real* Harriet, hop on over to my blog https://ladiesindefiance.com/2018/02/14/she-was-really-hell-bent-on-blessings/ and finish reading this short post about her.

She did, indeed, drive wagons with her sons and open a grand resort with her daughter, but her story is about dreams coming true. While you're visiting my blog, maybe you'll follow me. I've got a lot of stories there like this one. I love these stout-hearted women.

Oh, and one last thing. I took a little historical license with a few facts for this story, including stagecoach and wagon driver Charly Parkhurst. *She* didn't actually make it to California until 1851, a year after my story was set. I felt in a way this was her story, too, though, and wanted to include her. She proved a woman could drive a freight wagon just as good as a man—even if she had to pretend to be a man to do it! If you'd like to learn a little about Charly, you can check out my short blog on her at https://ladiesindefiance.com/2014/05/15/charly-parkhursts-legendary-life-of-lies/. If you'd like to meet all the authors in this series, pop over to our readers page https://www.facebook.com/groups/LoveMorePreciousThan Gold/ on Facebook. We'd love to meet you there, too!

Well, till next time, happy trails and may the Lord bless and keep you!

A LOOK AT: LOCKET FULL OF LOVE

A woman he can't forget. A man she can't forgive. A key hidden in a locket will send them on a journey of revelation...and romance.

Ten years ago, Captain Robert Hall saved Juliet Watts from a brutal Indian raid—only to lose her just as quickly. Now an intelligence officer, Robert finally finds her again in St. Joseph, Missouri, hardened by grief and anger over the senseless death of her husband, who perished retrieving a simple gold locket.

But the locket was no trinket.

When a hidden key and cryptic message are discovered inside, Juliet and Robert are thrust into a tangled web of wartime secrets, political conspiracy, and buried truths. As they journey to uncover the locket's true purpose, long-buried emotions begin to surface— forcing Juliet to confront her past and Robert to reckon with the promise that's kept him searching all these years.

But powerful forces will do anything to keep those secrets hidden... even if it means silencing them forever.

Locket Full of Love is a sweeping historical romance filled with heart-pounding mystery, second chances, and the healing power of truth.

AVAILABLE SEPTEMBER 2025

ABOUT THE AUTHOR

Heather Blanton is a *USA Today* bestselling author of thirty Christian Western romances, including the highly rated and awarded Romance in the Rockies series. She is also an award-winning script writer. Her Romance in the Rockies series has been optioned for a limited TV series, and her script *Unbridled Hearts* is currently optioned as well.

She grew up in the mountains of Western North Carolina on a steady diet of *Bonanza, Gunsmoke,* and John Wayne Westerns. Her daddy taught her to shoot when she was five, and she can hit that at which she aims.

Her novels are all Christian Western romance because she enjoys creating feisty pioneer women who struggle to find love and hold on to their faith. Like all good, old-fashioned Westerns, there is always justice, a moral message, American values, lots of high adventure, unexpected plot twists, and often a touch of suspense.

www.authorheatherblanton.com